THINNING THE TURKEY HERD

About a month ago she asked me to look into something for her. She says to me, "You have a nose for mayhem."

I says, "Maybe I got a nose, but I ain't got the stomach."

"Well," she says, "if you would, I'd like you to ask around. Someone's thinning the turkey herd."

I says, "How's that?"

She says, "You know how cops talk about gonifs and jinkey men, and lawyers talk about deep pockets? In the modelling business they talk about the turkey herd – hundreds of pretty girls posing in bathing suits and underwear hoping to get famous. They pour into town every year. Too many for the marketplace. It thins them out. This season someone's thinning them out the hard way. Three pretty out-of-town would-be models have been found dead so far."

I says, "How come it ain't plastered all over the papers?"

She says, "The police don't think they're connected and dead women are found in Chicago nearly every day."

I ask around, but that's all I do. Now she's at my door and she don't even have to tell me what she's here about.

Also by the same author, and available from Coronet Crime:

THE CAT'S MEOW

About the author

Robert Campbell is a successful writer of novels, screenplays, and television plays. His screenplay, *The Man of a Thousand Faces*, was nominated for an Academy Award. His mystery, *In La-La Land We Trust* was chosen as the best crime novel of 1986 by *The Washington Post*. The first novel in his Jimmy Flannery mystery series, *The Junkyard Dog*, won an Edgar Award. Robert Campbell lives in Carmel, California.

Thinning The Turkey Herd

A Jimmy Flannery Mystery

Robert Campbell

CORONET BOOKS
Hodder and Stoughton

First published in Great Britain in 1990 by Coronet paperbacks

Coronet Crime edition 1990

British Library C.I.P.

Campbell, R. Wright (Robert Wright),
1927–
Thinning the turkey herd.
I. Title
813.54 [F]

ISBN 0 340 53035 9

The characters and situations in this book are entirely imaginary and bear no relation to any real person or actual happenings.

Printed and bound in Great Britain for Hodder and Stoughton Paperbacks, a division of Hodder and Stoughton Ltd., Mill Road, Dunton Green, Sevenoaks, Kent TN13 2YA. (Editorial Office: 47 Bedford Square, London WC1B 3DP) by Cox & Wyman Ltd., Reading, Berks.

For Jane Chelius

1

About a month and half ago, the end of March, ex-mayor Jane Byrne is on TV. Out there in her trench coat during a storm what's churning up the lake. There's waves washing over Lake Shore Drive for the first time in living memory. She's acting fighting mad and asking just what the mayor intends to do when the *real* rains come in April and May if he's just ". . . sitting in his office doing nothing" at the moment.

I don't think there's anyplace but Chicago where a candidate in the primaries would stand up and accuse the incumbent of being helpless in the face of God.

You got to remember that Jane beat the Machine in seventy-nine—which was not the first time the know-it-alls said the Machine was busted and rusted—over that business about ex-mayor Bilandic not clearing the snow. But she was very quick to embrace the old pols and play kissy-face with them even before she sat down in the mayor's chair.

Now she's hoping she can grab the rain as her issue and use it, not only to beat the man in city hall, but to beat every other player in the game.

While she's out there getting wet, the rest of them are staying inside keeping dry and thinking up dirty tricks.

There's even a rumor that the incumbent is going to run Independent and short-circuit the Cook County Democratic organization, run by Ray Carrigan, once and for all.

Democrats is switching parties to run in the Republican primary.

There's even talk of making the mayor's race nonpartisan this election. But nobody's paying much attention to that notion since its biggest booster is the late Hizzoner's son and heir, who's also tying on his track shoes one more time.

I've got my own ideas about who I'd like to see sitting on the fourth floor, but when the primaries are over I'll be working for the election of whoever the Democratic candidate turns out to be. The reason is because my family has been Democrats as far back as there's been Flannerys in Chicago. My old man was a fireman and a very active precinct captain. I work for the Sewer Department and I'm a precinct captain too. In the Twenty-seventh, which is close to the heart of the town and has a little of everything going for it.

I got to say one thing about what's a precinct captain. Some people think it means I'm a cop. I'm not a cop. I'm a worker for the party. I get out there and knock on doors around election time, but mostly I'm there in case somebody in my precinct needs a helping hand. This morning this old lady, Mrs. Seidman, stops me on the street and says, "You promised."

"If I promised, I'll make good, Mrs. Seidman," I says. "You mind kicking my memory in the shins a little bit?"

"The tree."

I don't remember her saying anything to me about a tree. But if she remembers a tree, but forgets she never said anything to me about it, I'm not going to tell her she's mistaken and make her feel like maybe she's getting senile or is getting that disease my wife tells me about. That Alzheimer's. That disease what sounds as bad as anything can be.

"My shin could use another kick," I says.

"The limb. The tree with the limb what blocks the sun

from my porch in the morning where I sit and have my tea and banana."

"Oh, *that* tree," I says. Sometime ago another old Jewish lady asked me for a similar favor and I forgot to do it and then she was killed. Getting tree limbs cut off so they should have a little sun in the kitchen or *not* letting them get cut so the sun shouldn't fade the linoleum makes up the bulk of the requests I get from the old people in my precinct, so you can understand I sometimes forget who asked for what and which tree is which. "What about that tree, Mrs. Seidman?"

"Well, the limb's still there, ain't it?" she says, surprised at how dumb a young person like myself can be. "You promised me you'd have some men over, they should trim it so I can get the sun."

"You live on the third floor, second house from the corner, west side of the street?"

"You got it. Such a memory," she says. "See if you can make it work long enough to get that tree cut."

"I'll do that, Mrs. Seidman," I says.

She goes into Joe and Pearl Pakula's grocery store, which is in the downstairs corner of the building where I live with my wife, Mary, on Polk Street.

"Just enough to give me a little sun with my tea and banana," she says from the doorway. "Not too much. It shouldn't be a bare stick."

So, I help people like that. Or see that a sick kid gets to the clinic when the mother and father are both working and can't make it. Or I see the water gets turned on when they can't pay the bill because the old man's out of work and the toilet won't flush. Or I talk to the assistant DA when some damn fool kid gets hisself in trouble which could only make him worse if he's tossed in Juvenile Hall. Sometimes I work it the other way around and see to it that some really vicious young animal gets put in the slammer, where he won't be able to terrorize his neighbors.

I'm very conservative. I want things to be the same next year as they was this year. Maybe a little better, but not different. I don't like different. I don't like change. I like good things to be passed from hand to hand in an orderly fashion. That's why I work for the party candidate. I'm not out to lead no crusades. I'm out to protect my neighborhood.

That's not what my wife, Mary, says. She says all anybody has to do is go "Ouch!" and I'm ready to put on my white armor and pick up my sword and go out looking for dragons.

She also tells me I could do a lot more if only I'd take the offer my chinaman—which is like what you'd call a patron—makes to me about the first of every month or whenever I see him, whichever comes soonest. Chips Delvin has been around so long there's them what says he really died a long time ago but somebody stuffed him and works him with strings. He wants me to be the ward boss of the Twenty-seventh. He used to be the alderman, too, until a lipstick lesbian by the name of Janet Canarias snatched that away from him. Delvin and the boys wanted me to run against her, but I wouldn't and Delvin never completely forgave me about that.

My Mary's not all that interested in politics, she's a nurse over to Passavant, but now that we're married I notice she acts a lot like I've seen wives act ever since I was old enough to notice. They can't seem to keep from beating the donkey with a stick, wanting him to go farther and faster, "for his own good."

In fact we're sitting at the supper table right after I make a call to get a crew over from Parks and Recreation, Shade Tree Division, about Mr. Seidman's tree, and Mary's saying, "It's not for me, James" (she's the only person what calls me James, just like my mother—God rest her soul—used to call me), "it's for yourself."

"You'll pardon me, sweetheart," I says, "but I don't

see how taking on a job I don't want to take on and giving up one I like is doing anything for me."

"For one thing," she says, "being ward leader, you can make certain you never have to go walking through the sewers ever again."

"Well," I says, "that was just one of those things. Chairman Carrigan wanted to give me a slap on the wrist because I took away his face at the Democratic Party Solidarity Dinner. He gives the word to Dunleavy, down at Streets and Sanitation, who puts the arm on Delvin. So what happened is an accident."

"It's the kind of accident you should protect yourself against. Also, there's not a reason in the world why you can't take over Delvin's job as sewer boss when he hands over the job of ward leader to you."

"And get pinned down behind a desk?"

"You know and I know that Delvin's never even in his office. He stays at home with his feet up in front of the fire while Mrs. Banjo serves him whiskey in a teacup."

"You wouldn't want me to do that, now, would you?" I says, cracking a grin, but not getting one back.

"Don't get Irish with me. I notice, the older you get, you're looking less and less like Jimmy Cagney."

"So I've lost me charm?" I says.

She gets up, rushes over and kisses me while I've still got a mouthful of tuna casserole.

We're having the canned peaches with cream on top when there's a knock on the front door.

When I go to open the door it's Alderman Canarias standing there looking very bad.

About a month ago she asked me to look into something for her. She says to me, "You have a nose for mayhem."

I says, "Maybe I got a nose, but I ain't got the stomach."

"Well," she says, "if you would, I'd like you to ask around. Somebody's thinning the turkey herd."

I says, "How's that?"

She says, "You know how cops talk about gonifs and jinkey men, and lawyers talk about deep pockets? In the modeling business they talk about the turkey herd—hundreds of pretty girls posing in bathing suits and underwear hoping to get famous. They pour into town every year. Too many for the marketplace. It thins them out. This season somebody's thinning them out the hard way. Three pretty out-of-town would-be models have been found dead so far."

I says, "How come it ain't plastered all over the papers?"

She says, "The police don't think they're connected and dead women are found in Chicago nearly every day."

I ask around, but that's all I do. Now she's at my door and she don't even have to tell me what she's here about.

She makes a sound like a cough which I know is a mouthful of strangled tears and says, "A friend of mine is missing."

2

Janet Canarias is a Latino, Puerto Rican, whatever, with the blackest hair, whitest teeth, and flashingest eyes I ever seen. Besides which she wears bright red lipstick outlined with darker lines which can't help but make a healthy man wonder what it'd be like to kiss her. Right now she prefers women for companions but there was a time when she slept with men. "And may do again, Flannery, if Mary should ever up and leave you," she likes to tease.

I can't understand how some people can be so definite about how having sex this way or that, worshiping God this way or that, or eating your peas with a fork or a knife makes one way right and the other wrong. Except you can't get many peas to your mouth balancing them on a knife.

Janet is smart and honest and a good friend. That's what counts.

She looks a lot smaller than she usually looks sitting there at our kitchen table with her red-tipped fingers holding on to the coffee mug which she always takes instead of a cup and saucer.

"Wait a minute," I says. "You say your friend was supposed to be at your place but she wasn't there when you got home from the office? She's been gone overnight and you're already in a panic?"

"A night and a day. If Mary left Passavant but didn't

come home that night and all the next day, wouldn't you be frantic?"

"Sure, but we're married and . . ." I bit my tongue. "That didn't come out the way I meant it. I mean we live together. I'm not saying that you and your friend don't worry about each other just as much as . . ."

"I know what you're saying. You're saying that you think what I have with Joyce is casual. We're both free to come and go as we please, so what's the fuss."

"I didn't mean that she was off having a one-nighter with somebody," I said, backpedaling like crazy and just getting myself stuck deeper in the mess I was making.

"Jimmy, Jimmy," Mary says, reaching over to take my hand, "you're going to knock your teeth out tripping over your tongue." She leans toward Janet. "We don't know Joyce, do we? You've never told us about her."

Janet leans back in her chair and takes a breath, calming herself because she knows that up to now words have just been rattling out of her mouth without making much sense. Mary's looking for a starting point so we can take it one step at a time.

"You ever feel like they're changing the rules on us almost every hour on the hour?" Janet says.

"Whoosh," I says. Mary nods her head and grins lopsided.

"Sometimes I feel like the brakes are gone and I'm afraid to put my foot on the ground to try and stop the wagon because it'll burn my shoe off," Janet says. Then she shakes herself and says, "Okay. I met Joyce Lombardi six months ago. I was asked to make an appearance at the auto show and I thought it would be good public relations. I meant to stay half an hour. I stayed for three, angling to meet this beautiful blond girl who was draping herself over the hood of a red car that was advertised to go a hundred and sixty miles an hour in ten seconds from a standing start. Joyce saw me staring at her and winked at me, letting me know she thought it was a lot of damned foolishness too, but it was a job and helped to pay the rent. Later on, when we were sitting together in the courtesy booth having a coffee during her break she said, 'Men'll get you laying down one way or another, won't they? Well, I'd rather get paid for draping myself on a sports car than a bed.'

"I could tell she was just coming off a bad experience with some boyfriend or live-in. I didn't question her, but she knew that I knew.

"She said, 'They've been giving you a lot of trouble too, haven't they? I read the papers and they tried to ruin you because you aren't gaga over them. Right?'

" 'Well, no. They don't like it that I prefer women, but all the mud they slung was at the lesbian only because she was also a politician looking to break their legs.'

"When she laughed it squeezed my heart. You've got to understand, I've had my share of men and women, but I never slept around. Yin or yang, I was never an alley cat."

Mary glances at me. "Yin is the passive female cosmic element and yang . . ."

"I'm not altogether uninformed about Chinese dualistic philosophy," I says in a voice which puts her in her place. Janet don't seem to notice the aside.

"That's not to say I was always looking for forever with every person I got involved with. Now this AIDS is turning a lot of heads around. There's plain good sense in finding out if a relationship can travel a long road before skipping off with somebody. So, I wasn't there to take advantage of Joyce because she was feeling badly. I wasn't looking for a score. It was three months before we touched."

I know she don't mean holding hands. Everybody's got their own delicacies no matter how up-front they are about most things.

"I think Joyce found her real self in the relationship just as I did a long time ago with an older woman," Janet goes on. "I asked her to come share my place. She wanted a little time to think about it. She was supposed to call me yesterday afternoon and say yes or no."

"But she don't call," I says.

Her eyes fill up. "No, she called and said she'd move in before dark. I had a desk full of paper. She had a key to my apartment, so I told her to take a suitcase of her things home and we'd move the rest of her stuff out of her place over the weekend. When I got home about seven her suitcase was in the middle of the living-room floor, a tape was playing on the deck, but she wasn't there. When she still wasn't back by nine I called her apartment and got her answering machine. She'd put a new message on it."

"What was the message?"

The tears spill over and run down her cheeks. "It referred all calls to my number."

By the time it's midnight and Joyce still don't come home to Janet's, Janet gets in her car and drives over to the converted loft over on Morgan, just off West Washington, where Joyce has her place. She knocks on the door more than once but gets no answer. She's got no key to the apartment like Joyce has a key to hers, because Joyce never offered and Janet never pushed for it. She hammers some more until the person what lives next door gets up and comes out to see what the hell the racket's all about. Janet says that she's looking for her friend. The neighbor, who turns out to be Joyce's landlord, says he hasn't seen her for a couple of days.

Janet asks for a key. After some hemming and hawing the landlord says all right, he'll open the door for her, but Joyce better not be there doing it with somebody because if she is Janet will have to take the heat.

Well, Joyce ain't in there. The place looks like it always looked the few times that Janet was invited to visit.

"I went back home," Janet says. "I didn't know what

else to do. I tried to think about what could have happened. The best answer I kept on getting was that after she brought the suitcase to my place Joyce got the shakes. We'd made it clear what sort of a commitment we were getting into. Maybe, all of a sudden, she wanted to get away from my things, my smell, my music on the tape deck, and think it over. So she went out for a walk and ended up in a cocktail lounge. When two-thirty came and she still wasn't home I changed that to an all-night movie."

"When did you start calling the hospitals?" Mary says.

"About five o'clock this morning."

"And there was nobody who could possibly fit Joyce's description?"

"None that were unidentified. Not at the morgue either."

"Have you been to the police?" I says.

"I went to Missing Persons."

"And they told you they didn't start looking until after forty-eight."

She nods. "Then I went to see Captain Pescaro."

"He tells you he's not supposed to move until Missing Persons adds her name to the register."

"I asked the favor."

"So, the cops are out looking?"

"But I don't know how hard. That's why I want you to look, Jimmy."

3

I could've waited until morning, but Janet was so upset I thought I'd make some motions just so she'd calm down a little, knowing whatever could be done was being done.

Mary and me have supper early, so it was only six-thirty when I caught the El over to Morgan and West Washington.

It's a kind of mixed-up piece of town. There's plenty of empty lots with bent and busted chain-link fences falling down around empty lots, pads of concrete capping basements where buildings was supposed to have gone up but never did, warehouses, mostly for paper products, and building with offices, mostly for graphic designers and printers. There's some small warehouse conversions and a few beautiful old brick buildings that once was the mansions of the rich. It's a very quiet district after dark. A district you wouldn't really want to take a stroll around by yourself.

I make a beeline for the five-story building where Joyce has her place. It's sitting all by itself with empty space all around. There'd be good views of the city from the top floor.

The developer's put a fancy brass-and-glass door in front to sweeten up the building's face. There's imitation marble on the walls and floors in the little lobby, but it looks like he runs out of steam and money when it comes to the elevator. It's just an old factory cab. The directory alongside the beat-up painted doors tells me the bottom floor's occupied by a zipper manufacturer, the second floor by a photographer, half of the third looks to be empty and the other half is somebody's apartment. The fourth floor's got four apartments, 4A, B, C, and D. All occupied. The top's got three, a P, for "Penthouse" I suppose, One, Two, and Three. If you can afford the top floor you get a number instead of a letter. Don't ask me why.

The elevator's got a sign on it that says it only works with a key after ten o'clock at night and there's a heavy steel scissor gate, also on a lock, that blocks the staircase unless you got a key after midnight.

There's canvas on the walls of the elevator and a twenty-five-watt bulb recessed overhead in a well without a pane of glass. I punch the button for the penthouse and the elevator starts off like an old man jumping out of bed, coughing and sputtering all the way to the top until it bangs into the keepers.

I get out in a corridor with worn and cracked industrial tile on the floor, expecting to find it empty. Instead I see this little man with a fox terrier at his feet, a furry creature in his arms, and what looks like a snake draped around his neck. He's creeping down the hall all bent over sideways with his ear next to the wall. He's listening so hard he don't even seem to hear the elevator coming up and the door opening, which is a sound what could wake the dead. But when I take a step, quiet as you please, he whips around like he expects a mugger.

"Hey," I says, "you don't mind my asking, but is that a snake around your neck?"

He blinks at me, don't say a word, then scuttles down the stairs. I hurry over but he isn't stopping. He goes pattering down, keeping to the walls just like a rat.

I walk down the hall to a small window at the end, passing P Three on my right. There's a line of light under the door. At the end of the hall P Two's on my right and

P One's on my left. There's another door next to the one to P Two. I try the knob and it opens onto a flight of service steps. The window looks out on a hell of a view of the east side of Chicago.

I go to the door of P Two. It's painted orange. There's a brass door knocker like two hands shaking with some ribbons flying around them underneath a peephole and a little brass frame with a calling card in it that says "J. Lombardi." There's also a hand-printed note tacked under the doorbell what says the bell don't work. I knock on the off chance that between the time Janet stops by the house and tells me her problem until I get where I am, Joyce has decided to come home. Nothing happens. I knock again and put my ear to the door in case I can hear any whispers or footsteps.

I got my ear stuck to the door when somebody says, "I hope you're with the rat catcher or I'm going to have to split your skull."

I turn my head, but I don't turn my body, not wanting whoever it is to think I'm making a move and clobber me.

There's a monster standing there, six-feet-five if he's an inch, three hundred and ten if he's a pound. He's got a small ax in his hand and a worried look on his face and I'm wondering why Janet didn't warn me about this sucker, who I figure is the landlord she told me about.

"Rat catcher?" I says.

"Willy Dink."

"No, I'm not with Willy Dink. I'm looking for Ms Lombardi."

"You know Joyce?"

"Well, no, I don't know Ms Lombardi, but I promised somebody I'd look around and try to find out how come she didn't show up at a place last night where she was supposed to show up."

"You're not the only one looking for Joyce."

"You mean Ms Canarias, the lady who talked to you last night? She's the one I'm helping out."

"Okay then," the giant says, "but there's been others looking for her too."

"Today?"

"All day."

"How many?"

"At least two I know about. I don't hang around the house all day long, you know. I got things to do."

"Do you suppose you could put down that ax and let me come in and sit down?"

"What for?"

"I'd like to ask you a few questions."

"I don't even know who you are," he says.

"My name's Jimmy Flannery and now you're one up on me."

"I heard about you, Flannery. Something about a gorilla. Or was it an alligator?"

"It was both."

He tucks the ax handle in his armpit and sticks out his paw. My hand gets lost in it while he tells me his name is Hymie Kropotkin and won't I come in and have a glass of tea.

There's a samovar on the table right in front of the biggest window in his loft and it looks like he's always got it on the boil. While he's pouring tea I take a seat in one of the canvas deck chairs he uses for living-room furniture.

"I can only tell you what I told the lady. I don't have no idea where Joyce could be. I don't understand what the fuss is all about. Joyce is old enough to stay out all night if she wants."

"Well, that's just it, don't you know. She was supposed to stay all night with Miss Canarias."

He sets the tea down on the cable reel he uses for a coffee table and stares at me with shrewd eyes. He sits down in his deck chair. For a second I think it's going to give way, then I see the struts is twice as heavy and the canvas twice as thick as the one I'm sitting in. He takes a swallow of tea. I try to do the same but it's so hot it burns my lips so I don't even take a sip. He sighs like a train coming into a station and looks at the ceiling for a second.

"You mean what I think you mean?" he says.

I nod.

"I wondered," he says, kind of sad. "Beautiful girl like that should have had a hundred men buzzing around."

"I think maybe she had a boyfriend. This other thing is recent," I says.

He sighs again and says, "What's the difference to me? I'd've never had a chance even if she was a nymphomaniac."

"You know the two men who came looking for Miss Lombardi today?" I says, dropping the Ms because he's not a man to worry about such things and I don't want to press the point.

"One was a woman. Not the Canarias woman. Some woman who's been around once or twice before."

"They didn't come together, did they?"

"No. The man came first. This morning around eleven. The woman came around about one this afternoon. The man came again around three and again at six."

I'm thinking he sees a lot for not hanging around all day.

"Did you talk to them? Did you ask them what they wanted?"

"It wasn't none of my business. I saw them through the peephole I got in the door."

"You do that whenever somebody comes visiting Miss Lombardi?"

His eyes get like a couple of slits in an iron mask. "Some lady comes around in the wee hours asking where Miss Lombardi's got to. I don't see Miss Lombardi all day. Naturally I'm worrying. Every time I hear the elevator, I take a look. That's only natural."

He's getting formal on me, calling her Miss Lombardi

instead of Joyce the way he's been doing, so I know he's losing his temper and that he's meaning to tell me that his relationship with her was strictly rents and leases.

"Sure, it's only natural," I says. "I wasn't saying that. . ."

"I know what you wasn't saying and what you're thinking. You're thinking I'm a busybody sonofabitch what took every chance he could to cop a peek at the beautiful girl what lived next door."

He was getting red in the face. I went shush-shush, not wanting him to get mad at me, and said, "Mr. Kropotkin, I'm just asking questions. I'll be asking a lot more of just about everybody I meet around here if Miss Lombardi don't turn up. Could you tell me did you know the man?"

He shook his head. "Never seen him before."

"Do you know the woman's name?"

"We was never introduced," he says with a twisty lip.

"I understand. Did the elevator come up to this floor anytime last night or today, while you were home, but when you took a look you didn't see anybody?"

"A couple of times. I was on the crapper once." He glares at me like I'm getting personal. "I figured it was Willy Dink. He's been up and down these floors and halls fifty times a day for the last week. Sometimes I see him, sometimes I don't."

"Is Willy Dink really a rat catcher?"

"Rats, mice, cockroaches, ants."

"Ants?"

"He's got hisself a little thing he calls an armadillo." He holds out his hands the size of a big cat. "About this big. He'll rent it out to you, you got trouble with ants in the kitchen."

"What does he rent you for cockroaches?"

"I never had them, so I never asked."

"You think sometimes when the elevator came up it was somebody for the person who lives in P Three?"

"I doubt it. Mr. Scanlan ain't been home for a couple of weeks."

"Oh?"

"He travels."

"Doing what?"

"Selling costume jewelry. Stuff like that."

"How about the tenants on the fourth floor? They at home?"

"There ain't no tenants on the fourth floor. I ain't finished the remodel yet."

"There's names on the directory downstairs."

"I got the space on the third for rent. I don't want people coming to look at the third to know the fourth floor is empty. Some people are scared to live in a half-empty building."

"But you've got somebody on the third?"

"That's right. I got half the third, a big apartment, all rented out. To Mrs. Warren. She's a widow. You wouldn't be interested in the other half, would you? It's beautiful space."

"I'm sure it is," I says, "but I don't think my wife would want to live in a half-empty building."

"I never should've told you about the fourth floor," he says.

"Anyway, we really like the place we got."

"Oh, sure."

I take out one of the file cards I carry around with me and a ball point pen with red ink.

"So let me get this straight in my head," I says. "The first floor's for business. The photographer lives on the second floor?"

"His name's Jerry Miller. This place is supposed to be just his studio. He's got a house over in Evanston, but he must be having trouble with the wife because he sleeps here more than he sleeps there."

"Mrs. Warren on the third. Nobody on the fourth. Just

you and Miss Lombardi on the fifth because Scanlan's been away."

"What are you going to do with those names?"

"Just talk to the people who belong to them."

"Well, I don't know if I want you bothering my tenants."

"Miss Lombardi stays missing another night, you and them are going to be talking to the cops. Talking to me could be good practice."

"Well, you'll do what you want, I guess," he says and starts getting to his feet, which is something to see.

I thank him for the tea.

"I may have a couple more questions for you later on," I says after he herds me to the door.

"Well, maybe I'll answer them and maybe I won't."

"Any chance of me having a look inside her apartment?"

"No chance at all."

"I didn't think so," I says and walk down the hall to the elevator. Then I walk back to P Three because the line of light ain't showing at the bottom of the door. This Scanlan, who ain't supposed to be home, could be home. But when I ring the bell and wait I get no answer.

I get on the elevator and ride it all the way to the bottom. Then I walk up to the third floor and ring the bell by Mrs. Warren's door.

From inside I hear the first half of "Meet Me in St. Louis" played on chimes.

4

When she opens the door I understand where they got that saying about the merry widow. Mrs. Warren's about fifty, give or take. The face and body don't show it but she's getting a little crepe on her chest and her hands won't lie about her age. Her hair's what was called platinum blond back in the thirties when Jean Harlow made it popular. I think it's natural. Either that or she can afford bleach jobs as expensive as her face lifts. Her eyes are violet which surprises me because I thought Elizabeth Taylor had the patent on eyes that color. Her face is shaped like a heart with these violet eyes, a nose some women I know would kill for and a mouth like a valentine just the right distance under it.

"My name is Jim Flannery. I hate to bother you this hour of the night."

"Let me think about it, Jimmy. With that red hair you got, maybe I'll let you bother me."

"I've got a few questions I'd like to ask you."

"Oh, that kind of bother. Well, if that's what you've got in mind we can take care of it right out here." Then she grabs me by the sleeve and says, "I'm being funny. Come on in."

Expensive dye jobs, expensive face lifts, expensive decorators. Whoever did the place liked white, thick and shiny. Chairs, rugs, and tables. Also big spots of color here and there which could be a pillow, could be a framed print, could be a big jar full of flowers, or could be the sheer floor-length curtains in geometric designs which she uses for room dividers.

She should have been wearing a white satin sheath, a sheer negligee with marabou trim, and feathered high-heeled mules. She's wearing felt carpet slippers and one of those bathrobes what look like they was made out of a horse blanket.

"You want something to drink? I'm having cocoa," she says.

"Cocoa would do me fine."

"You sit in the living room. That's those two chairs and a couch with the steel coffee table by the window. I should hand out diagrams."

She goes behind one of the long curtains. A light goes on but I don't see her touch a switch. Behind the sheer squares, triangles, and circles of the curtain I can watch her making cocoa in the fanciest kitchen I ever see.

From where I take a seat in one of the big white chairs I can look out this huge picture window at the place where the Chicago River and the South Branch come together. Where the Insurance Exchange building is.

When she steps through the curtains again she's carrying a tray with mugs of cocoa with big marshmallows melting on top. Also some napkins and a plate of cookies.

"How did you do the lights?" I says.

"Ain't that something?" she says. "There's a pressure strip all around it. All you got to do is step on it and the lights go on."

"Suppose somebody's already in there with them on and somebody else walks in there and turns them off?"

"Then you got to tap dance. So, how do you like it?"

"The cocoa?"

"It's the real thing. Not that instant stuff. You notice I made it with a marshmallow just like your mother used to do?"

"How do you know that?"

She smiles but don't say. Instead she says, "I meant how do you like the apartment."

"It cost plenty."

"I had a couple of rich husbands."

"Divorced?"

"Dead."

"So you're all alone?"

She sat back and looked me over. "You're not. You're married."

"Yes, I am. How can you tell?"

"You learn," she says, and buries her little nose in the mug of cocoa.

"Ain't you afraid, letting a stranger in?"

"You ever meet Hymie, owns this building? Lives upstairs?"

"I just talked to him."

"I always know when he's home. We've got an arrangement. I'm a believer in electrical wonders. I think I'm in any trouble, he comes running with his little ax."

"How do you make him come?"

"Well, hell, the regular way." She grins. "You mean how do I make him come running?" She shakes her head. "Let me just tell you I can work it from anyplace in the joint."

With all this talk of possible danger to a lady living on her own, she ain't the least bit nervous or concerned, even if she has got an ogre standing by. Anybody really wanted to do her, she'd be dead before Hymie made it down the stairs. But she's not worried. She just sits there sipping her cocoa and looking at me with those violet eyes.

"I didn't mean to bring up a subject that could scare you," I says.

"It don't scare me. Aren't you listening?"

"I meant I was just wondering if all the ladies what live in this building feel as safe as you do."

"There's only one other lady living in this building. That's Joyce Lombardi, on the fifth."

"I know."

"That who you're nosing around about? Figures. Married or not, with that red hair . . ."

"It's nothing like that. Did she have the same kind of arrangement with Hymie that you got?"

"I wouldn't know. I doubt it. I doubt if she'd make the arrangement with Hymie that I made with Hymie. But he'd keep an eye on her all the same. He's a peeper. Got himself a telescope and looks at the apartment houses along the river."

Her stare's as level as a ruler. She's waiting for me to go on. When I don't she says, "So, is that all you want to know?"

"Are you very friendly with Joyce Lombardi?"

"What's very friendly? We chew the fat a little if we happen to meet in the laundry room downstairs or the elevator. She's been here for a meal more than once. She invited me into her place for a drink once or twice, but she always had someplace to go and I didn't stay long. We didn't exchange girlish confidences and I didn't try to be her mother."

"What kind of young woman is she?"

She frowns a little, then catches herself doing it and rubs it away with her fingertips. "I don't know, Red. I think I know women as well as I do men. But about Joyce Lombardi I don't know. She keeps to herself as far as I can tell."

"No visitors?"

"How would I know? I live on the third. She lives on the fifth. In a building nowadays you've got no neighbors."

"How does she make the rent on a penthouse apartment?" I says.

"Well, that's the point, isn't it? I've had plenty but I'm not living in a penthouse apartment."

I don't mention that she's living in one probably twice as big.

"Somebody was keeping her?"

"That's a nice old-fashioned phrase. Next thing you know, you'll be calling it a love nest."

We sit there thinking about old-fashioned things for a minute.

"So, that's all I can tell you, Red. Joyce and I weren't friends, just city neighbors. No confessions, no consultations. You want some more cocoa?"

"What I already drank is making me sleepy."

"Want me to tuck you in?" She laughs again and says, "You've got a marshmallow mustache."

I wipe my top lip with one of the napkins.

"If you're finished with your cocoa and you don't want anything . . . else, I guess it's time for me to ask you to leave so I can go to bed and get my beauty sleep."

I don't want to push it so I get up and let her walk me to the door.

"Next time you want to ask me any questions," she says, "use the telephone first. I got nicer things than this old flannel robe. Things that go better with the furniture."

I smile and tell her I'll do that. Then I says, "One more thing?"

"I'm listening."

"How come you didn't ask me was I a cop?"

She smiles and winks at me. "Are you a cop?" she says.

After she closes the door on me, I walk down the hall and take the stairs to the second floor.

I ring the bell just in case the photographer, Jerry Miller, is sleeping at the office again instead of at home. There's no answer and the pebbled glass set in the door stays dark.

I go down to the ground floor.

In the lobby I spot Willy Dink again, but he's through the door to the basement before I can get him to stand still.

5

When I get back home it's about nine o'clock. Janet's still there, sitting in the parlor with Mary, watching the television. The way they both look up at me with these glazed looks I know if I asked them what they was watching they couldn't tell me.

The hollows of Janet's eyes are dark like they've been stained.

"What can you tell me, Jimmy?"

"I don't think I can tell you anything. That monster what owns the building and me had a good talk, but if I learned anything about what could've happened to your friend, I don't know it yet. There's nobody on the first floor . . ."

"And you're going to give it forty-eight, just like the cops," she says, getting up out of the chair.

"You've got to understand, Janet, I've got no official capacity. I can't go around knocking on doors in the middle of the night . . ."

"It's nine o'clock. I don't think anybody over three years and under eighty is in bed yet." She goes out into the hall and takes her coat and scarf off the rack by the front door. "It's okay," she goes on. "I don't expect you to lose any sleep."

I'm right behind her. Mary stays where she is because she knows this is between me and Janet and third parties would only make it worse. I put my hand out and touch Janet on the shoulder like I'm ready to help her get her arm in her sleeve, but she jerks away from me. I step up close and put my arms around her. Her back's to me.

"Listen," I says. "I'd lose sleep if I thought it would do any good right now. I'd stick my hand in the fire. I don't even have a hint about where I should start."

She shakes her head and laughs. She's laughing at herself for getting mad at me. I understand she's so scared she's got to get mad at somebody. She relaxes and I let her go. When she turns around to face me, she's smiling like she's sorry. "Mary sees you grabbing me like that, she'd divorce you."

"Not if you're only playing," Mary says from the parlor. The next minute she's standing in the doorway to the hall, smiling at Janet. "You go home and get some sleep. If Joyce's all right, you'll be sorry you lost your sleep and let yourself look so bad. If she's not, you'll need all the strength you've got and then some."

"You sure you can drive?" I says.

"I came in a cab," Janet says.

"I'll run you home."

"Oh, no," she says, "I'll get one on the avenue."

"Oh, no, yourself. I'm driving you home."

I get my coat off the hook and give Mary a hug and a kiss on the cheek. "I want to have a look at Joyce Lombardi's suitcase," I says, "so if it takes me a little while, don't you worry."

On the way over to her apartment, Janet's quiet for a long time. Then she says, "It's very funny."

"What's very funny?" I says.

"Independent women. There comes a time when we still turn to a man for help."

"Independent men got to ask for a woman's help sooner or later too. Sex ain't all that happens between people. There's some things men do better and there's some things women do better. For one thing, we look at things in different ways."

She leans across the seat and kisses me on the cheek.

We talk politics and the upcoming primaries until we get to her apartment house.

In her living room Joyce's suitcase and garment bag are still sitting in the middle of the floor. There's some soft music playing on the hi-fi. It's like a day and a half ain't gone by and we just walked in to find that Joyce wasn't there like she was supposed to be.

"Is that the music that was playing when you came home last night?" I says.

"I haven't turned it off, I just turned it down. It's on automatic reverse."

I go over and shut if off. You can't hold on to a minute of time that way. When I turn around, Janet's standing there looking down at the suitcase with the garment bag draped over it. I go over and start to reach for it and Janet gives a little gasp.

"It's not admitting anything," I says. "It's just moving her luggage so I can have a look at it. Is that all right?"

She looks at me, very troubled. You don't give a stranger permission to poke around in somebody's personal belongings unless that person ain't going to be around to complain. Finally she makes a move with her hand which tells me it's okay.

I lay the garment bag over the back of the sofa and put the suitcase on the cushions. It's not locked. I open it up and start lifting out a couple of skirts, a pair of slacks, some blouses, transparent envelopes for panties, panty hose, a bra, ankle socks, a pair of silk pajamas, and some embroidered scuffs. There's a few scarves, a leather bag full of costume jewelry, a pair of heels in covers, and a small assortment of scarves and belts.

The other half of the suitcase is filled with all the jars, bottles, cans, and utensils women carry with them when they go off anywhere even for a day, besides the stuff they carry around with them in their handbags all the time. I'm not going to name everything because I don't even know what half the stuff is. I poke around a little bit and, except for a half-empty bottle of aspirin and some anithistamines, I don't see anything that could be called substance, illegal or otherwise.

"You see anything unusual about what she's got in here?" I says, stepping back so Janet can get a better look.

"Unusual? How unusual?"

"Well, I don't know. That's why I'm asking."

Janet gives the bag a going-over. She even opens up a couple of bottles and jars and gives them a sniff.

"Nothing out of the ordinary so far as I can tell," she says.

"How about is there something should be there that ain't there?"

She looks at me, trying to work out my meaning.

"Like, if I was going anywhere to stay, I'd take my electric razor, I wouldn't want to use anybody else's razor."

She has another look. When she straightens up she starts to shake her head, then widens her eyes a little. "Her hair dryer."

"You got a hair dryer here?"

"Naturally. But it's like you and your razor. A woman gets used to the weight and feel of her own hand dryer when she blow-dries her hair."

"You notice anything else missing?"

"A pair of earrings. I bought a new pair of rhinestone earrings the day before Joyce called to say she was coming to live with me. They were on my dressing table." Her face starts to crumple. "Joyce probably tried them on before she left." She catches herself.

"So, maybe at least we know a reason why she could've took off with the bag on the floor and the tape deck playing. She went home to get her hair dryer, expecting to be maybe half an hour."

When I get home, Mary hears my key in the lock and

comes to the door to take off the night chain. It's not something she'll usually do, putting it on when I'm only going to be out for a little while that early at night, so I know she's feeling some anxiety.

"Come into the living room and tell me what you found out," she says.

"I didn't find out much. There's a big gamoosh what looks like a character out of some horror film. He's got an ax to discourage any intruders. He's also one of those landlords who's always got his eye to the spyhole to see what's going on in the apartment across the hall. Joyce Lombardi's apartment."

"What did he tell you?"

"That she ain't been home for a day or so and that a couple of people besides Janet and me, a man and a woman, was looking for her today. He says he don't understand the reason for all the fuss. Joyce is a grown-up woman, so what's the difference she stays out all night. He says she ain't popular. For a beautiful girl she ain't got many men friends."

I don't mention that a few times Kropotkin talks about Joyce Lombardi in the past tense because I don't know what it could mean yet. It could be the way he talks or it could be something else.

"Down the hall, on the same floor, we got a traveling salesman by the name of Scanlan who's supposed to be out on the road but there's a light under his door."

"Night-light on a timer to keep thieves away," Mary says.

"The building's locked up tight after midnight. Even if it wasn't, it's not the kind of setup a casual burglar looking for a score would bother with or the kind of situation a professional would risk unless he knew there was something really worth it behind the door."

"So Scanlan might not be smart about things like that."

"On the third floor of the building there's a lady calls herself a widow who's an ex-hooker or madam if I ever seen one. She's got hair the color of Jean Harlow's and an apartment furnished to go with it. Almost all white like Mae West used to have, if you know what I mean."

"That's two movie stars in one breath," Mary says. "She must be something."

"She thinks Joyce is being kept."

"Or she could be hooking."

"What?"

"Well, not walking the streets or draping herself over a bar," she says. "More like a call girl. A lot of them won't take dates at home."

"How do you know so much about how they operate?"

She looks at me like I'm one of God's innocents and puts her hand on my cheek. "Flannery, I've been working Emergency for five years. Tell me what I don't know."

"Don't you think she'd have told Janet? They're ready to set up housekeeping together. She's ready to change her life."

"Maybe she isn't going to change her way of living," Mary says. "Maybe the arrangement between them is that they're together when they're together and apart when they're apart."

"All right, so it could be that maybe Joyce Lombardi's a working girl besides sitting on cars at auto shows," I says. "Or it could be she's got an arrangement with a couple, three married men. Or it could be she's got one really rich boyfriend pays the overhead and, love or no love, she gets second thoughts when she drops her bag at Janet's. She decides to take a walk or maybe check back with the boyfriend."

"Janet said that when she met Joyce, the girl was coming down off a bad relationship," Mary says.

"That's what I'm saying. He could've been the one didn't want to make the commitment or something. So she tells him he ain't welcome anymore, pay the rent or don't pay the rent."

"He takes some time to think about it," Mary picks it

up. "He decides he doesn't want to lose her so he calls her up and asks for a new start."

"She says no because she's just okayed moving in with Janet," I says. "She's gone far enough to pack a bag and taxi over to Janet's place."

"He calls her again and gets her machine with Janet's number on the message. So he gets her there."

"He asks her to meet him and she says no, it's over," I says.

"He begs for five minutes," Mary says.

"On neutral ground. In a public place. A drugstore or a bar."

"She says okay. Five minutes," Mary says.

"She don't even turn off the tape deck because she don't expect to be gone long."

"Then he gets her off somewhere and then . . ."

It's what we've been leading up to. What comes after "and then" is the bad part. Like ". . . and then he murders her."

"It could be he rushes her off to Bermuda or the Bahamas. Like that."

"Something romantic."

"To celebrate getting back together again."

"And she forgets all about Janet and her suitcase sitting in the middle of Janet's living room."

"So, what I've got to do is find the boyfriend," I says. "But who's the guy who came looking for her three times today? That sounds like it could be the boyfriend and he's still looking for her just like Janet is."

We sit there. We're so quiet I can hear the clock ticking on the mantel.

"Is there something you're not telling me?" Mary says.

"There was no hair dryer in her bag. She was nervous waiting for Janet. She could have remembered she left the dryer in her bathroom so it gave her an excuse to get moving, to do something, instead of just sitting there waiting. If her dryer's still at her apartment it could mean she never made it back to her place."

We're quiet again and the clock keeps on ticking.

"You want some cocoa?" Mary says.

"I had some cocoa," I says. "Mrs. Warren gave me some."

"I hope that's all she gave you," Mary says. Her eyes are wide like she's trying to keep from crying. Her mouth trembles in a half-smile. She's trying to make a little joke to hold back the fear she feels for Joyce and Janet and for every other woman in this crazy world.

6

We go to bed at eleven o'clock but I'm still awake at two. I try to get out of bed as easy as I can, but Mary's awake and sitting up before I got my socks on.

"Where are you going?" she whispers.

"Go back to sleep," I whisper back. I always wonder why people whisper like that when there's nobody else living in the house you could wake up. "I got to find out something for myself," I says in a regular voice.

"At this hour in the morning? It's not that safe wandering around that section of town this time of the morning."

"I'll take the car and I won't be wandering," I says. "If I don't get up and go, I'll just lay here all night staring at the ceiling and won't be good for much tomorrow."

"Can't I come with you?"

I buckle up my pants and sit down on the bed.

"That's crazy," I says.

"No, it's not. I could come with you. Maybe I'll see something you won't see. Maybe I'll get an idea you wouldn't get."

I can see she don't even believe the case she's making. I put my arms around her. Her skin smells like fresh bread and her hair smells like lemon and roses. The fine hairs at the back of her neck are damp from sleep. I know she don't really want to get up and get dressed and go out in the dark with me. She's just afraid to be left alone after the things we talked about.

"You're home," I says. "There's nothing to be afraid of here. We're on the third floor and there's a houseful of people would come in a second if they heard anybody slamming on the door. You double-lock the front door like you do when I'm out late other times. This is only going to be a couple hours. If it looks like longer, I'll give you a call."

"I'm being foolish," she says, kneading my back with her fine strong hands. "So go ahead, but make sure you don't get shot for a prowler."

I stand up and slip a black jersey over my head.

"And don't you go knocking on Mrs. Warren's door asking for cocoa," she says.

I give her another hug and a kiss, grab my pea jacket and knitted watch cap, and go to the front door. Mary's behind me. I hesitate a second. She reaches up to kiss me again and says she'll be all right, it's just a little feminine anxiety. Like that's nothing to be worried about. I wait outside the door until I hear her double-lock it, before padding down the stairs in my sneakers and getting into my car.

It seems like it makes a hell of a racket turning over, but it catches on the third try and I'm off through the sleeping city toward the loft building on Morgan off West Washington.

Along the way I think about the difference being a man and being a woman. A man living alone has got worries and anxieties, just like anybody. His house can be burgled, things stolen, stuff destroyed. He could be home when it happens and get beat up, killed, even raped. But there's not so much of that happens to make the average man wake up in a cold sweat night after night. Every time the paper headlines some new rapist on the loose, half the women in the city lose a week of sleep. Women got to live with this free-floating uneasiness almost all their lives. It's a rotten thing for them to have to go through and I wish there was something I could do about it.

I pull up in front of where Joyce Lombardi lives around a quarter to three. I park the car and don't bother to lock it. Any car thieves out this time of night ain't looking for a nine-year-old clunker. Give it another year it could maybe be a classic. Then I'll lock it.

I got nothing with me, in case I meet somebody what wants to do me harm, except a six-cell flashlight in a steel case. I walk around the building, being careful not to step in the dog turds all over the ground. One of them humps up and nearly scares me to death. A water rat goes running like hell through the weeds. By the time I circle the building once, I know there's thirty-three possible ways to get in. The zipper factory's got ten windows on each side plus six at the back. There's the back door, up six steps to the first floor, a door at the side for taking out the trash, and the one in front. There's four windows in the front, but when I take a closer look I can see they're fixed panes, so unless somebody wants to break them, you can include them out as a way in.

There's also a fire escape at the back. Somebody could jump up and bring down the ladder and maybe find a window open on one of the floors. They could even go up on the roof and come down through a skylight if they was acrobats.

The second time around I check the silver tapes on the window security. Three of the back windows and six of the windows on one side have been maintained. That's where the office is and anything valuable would be kept. As far as the owners of the business are concerned, anybody who wants can steal the machines in front. They could probably make a profit on the insurance.

So, I'm standing against the wall in the darkest place thinking how professional I am, working it out that now there's only *twenty-four* ways to get in. If I walk around long enough maybe I'll decide there's *no* way to get in and then I can go home and get back into bed with Mary. I'm stalling and I know it.

I walk through the front door. It's unlocked because it's no good fumbling with a key out in the open where anybody can see you and maybe attack you. Once inside the lobby you've got a chance to at least lock the outer door from inside and have time enough to unlock the elevator or the gate before anybody chasing you could bust through the heavy plate glass.

I read the signs again about what times the elevator and the gate are locked. I try the elevator and nothing happens. I rattle the scissor gate. It's like a rock. I walk over and try the door to the basement through which Willy Dink had ducked when I left the building that evening. It's locked. The Yale's on the automatic catch. I slip it with a plastic credit card. So much for fancy security. Some people think a lock's a lock. Some locks ain't locks.

A long flight of steps leads down into a cellar like a cave. The big oil furnaces what heat the building take up one whole corner. The place is built back when there was nothing but coal for heating and the smell of it is still in the walls. There's a laundry room with two washers and two dryers right next to the elevator doors.

I walk to the side door. Sure enough there's a very large dumbwaiter next to it. There'd be a service door on each floor. When the building was divided up, the dumbwaiter would end up in only one apartment on the fifth, fourth, and third. The way it was located that would mean Scanlan's, an empty, and Mrs. Warren's. Since they occupy the whole floor, the photographer and the zipper factory would naturally have access also. I open up the dumbwaiter but the cab's someplace upstairs and I don't want to start it up. It looks old and unused and could make a racket. I could have that big gamoosh, Kropotkin, chasing me with his ax.

Instead I go to the end of the cellar, where the panes

of glass in the back door look a little lighter than the rest of the wall. There's a narrow staircase which goes all the way up to the second floor with a landing but no exit on the first. The door at the top opens from my side so I don't need a key. I thumb the latch and I'm inside the building in the photographer's studio.

It feels like the backstage of a theater or a sound studio where they make movies. Lights are hanging overhead from pipes, some with what they call barn doors on them, some with filters of one kind or another. Other lights is on tripods. When I move the beam of the flashlight around it's like all the shadows moving along the floor and walls are skinny animals stalking me.

There's a set what is supposed to look like a snow-covered hill. I know enough that the merchandise for catalogs is photographed way in advance. With spring here, this is for next winter.

Over to one side there's a table covered with a black cloth for taking pictures of small objects. The rest of the setup is a puzzle to me, a camera on a tripod, a mirror clamped to another tripod, and what looks like a long piece of pipe, cabled to a black box on the floor, clamped to a third.

There's a door in the wall what encloses the staircase which I figure goes on up to the other floors. There's big doors along one side where props and equipment too big for the regular entrances can be raised and lifted by a pulley system fixed on a crane arm like they have in the lofts of barns. I go across the whole length of the studio and through a door into a reception area. I turn on the lights. I'm not taking much of a chance. I doubt this Miller is going to leave Evanston this time of night to come sleep in his studio. Anybody outside, any local graveyard-shift workers, any cops on patrol, would've seen lights on in the studio other times when maybe Miller couldn't sleep or got up to take a pee. If they bothered thinking about it, which they probably wouldn't.

I'm thinking all this to keep me from thinking about what I'm doing, which is called breaking and entering and which could get me sent to the slammer. Or, at least, could make me use up all the favors I got on my books and all I'd get for the next ten years.

Miller's got pictures all around the walls. Mostly they're pictures of merchandise and women posing for catalogs.

There's a secretary's desk by the window. It's got a telephone, some directories, a cheap desk set, and a typewriter on it. I sit down in the chair and open the drawers. The usual. Paper clips, rubber bands, one of them little gadgets what pulls staples out of paper, and all the other stuff you'd expect to find in an office desk. Except there ain't any Kleenex with lipstick smudges on it, or an extra compact, or a bottle of nail polish or any of the things you'd expect to find in the drawers of a desk a woman worked at.

I go through the next door. It's the biggest darkroom I ever seen. Neat as a pin. There ain't even any negatives drying on a string. They're all in a dust-proof dryer. All the chemical trays are drained and dry. There's boxes of wipes and paper hand towels spaced out all along the workbench.

There's a door which is locked. I figure it's full of supplies.

In the middle of the room there's a big light table. About a hundred eight-by-ten glossies of beautiful girls are spread out all over it like somebody'd been sorting through them, pushing them around, picking them up and tossing them back again any old way. Except for a little pile held together with a paper clip. Four photos, a blond, two brunettes, and a redhead, with the blond on top.

All of them are very beautiful girls, looking different from one another, but the same as one another, the way beautiful girls do, if you know what I mean. It's in the eyes. The satisfaction with themselves, like they know, push comes to shove, all they got to do is find a man with a wallet or a house and two chickens and they won't get cold and they won't get wet and they won't go hungry. Also a kind of challenge in their eyes, like if you ain't knocked out by what you see, who cares? Poor you. Go get your eyes tested.

I poke around in every closet and cabinet. I'm not even sure what I'm looking for.

I finally turn out the lights and make my way back to the staircase that goes upstairs. It lets me out in the hallway on the third. I walk on up to the fourth.

There's a couple of dryboard walls up, but the whole floor is still undivided. It smells like damp plaster and dry rot. I don't turn on the lights because Kropotkin could get up, look out the window, and see the windowsills downstairs lit up. I use the flash, making sure it don't spear out through the windows if I can help it. When I run it along the baseboards I can see why Willy Dink is creeping around the halls. Moving shadows, making little skittering noises, are piled up over by a closet.

I walk toward them. Some of them take a powder, disappearing out in the shadows and along the baseboards. A couple of the rats stare at me until the last minute, wondering whether they should stand and fight. Then they run away too and I'm left looking at a very large brown stain that comes out from under the door.

I don't really want to open it. Now I know what I'm looking for, a dead girl put away for safekeeping, but I don't really want to find her. I put my hand on the knob, thinking that it might be smarter all the way around if I got the phone and got the homicide cops over. While I'm running that over in my mind, my hand turns the knob and I pull open the door.

Thank God there's no body chopped to pieces in the closet. But there *is* a mess on a piece of plastic tarp what could have only come from a body.

There's a hell of a screech behind my back what almost

knocks me out of my shoes. I whip around with the flashlight in my hand. The beam lands in the corner where the scream comes from. The hair on the back of my neck goes up. A snake has got its mouth opened very wide and is swallowing this huge water rat.

Somebody clears his throat. I whip around with the light again. I'm a nervous wreck. Willy Dink is standing there grinning foolishly. He's got yellow eyes what sparkle in the flashlight beam.

"So, you found my bait," he says.

7

We're sitting on the floor in the rubble of construction, sharing his thermos of coffee and a couple of sweet rolls. I'm getting an education about vermin control.

"What's with the kishkas in the closet?" I says.

"I told you. Bait. Nothing brings rats out of the walls faster than the smell of blood. I buy pig guts by the pound over to the slaughterhouse." He holds up a dirty hand like a skinny paw. "Now, you've got your ferret. You've got your king snake. You've got your rat or fox terrier," he says, picking up his lecture.

He's got a shaded lantern on the floor between us. This animal what looks like a weasel is sitting on his shoulder eating crumbs from his fingers. The little dog is laying next to his leg, taking a nap. Every once in a while he opens one eye and looks at me, then closes it right away when I look back. The snake's crawled over and is laying by his other leg. Every once in a while there's a little ripple and this bulge, the rat, moves down its body a little bit.

"Take your snap traps," Willy Dink says, "breaks their necks. You think them little suckers don't get wise to that one? Ain't you ever see them take cheese out of a trap without springing it and practically leave a note telling you ha-ha? That's rats for you."

"Smarter than people."

"Much. Then you got your poisons."

"They work?"

"Sometimes they work, sometimes they don't work. Either way you're in trouble. Don't work and you got some very mean rats. If it works you could have dead rats in the walls. Either you got to tear out the walls or live with the smell until they turn into mummies. Who wants that?"

"Nobody."

"So you got gas. Tent the building and pump in the cyanide. Kills everything in the place. Rats, mice, voles, and spiders. Kills spiders. Now, spiders are good creatures. Why should anybody want to kill them?"

I know better than to tell him I got a fear of spiders more than I got a fear of rats. Whenever one shows up in the bathroom, which thank God ain't very often, Mary's got to kill it.

"Cyanide's in the walls and floors now. Who knows what it can do to you? Look at this asbestos. Everything's hunky-dory. We got asbestos in wallboard, tiles, even wallpaper. Then they find out it can kill you. Maybe they find out cyanide in the walls can kill you. What do you think?"

"I think maybe you could be . . ."

"Right. I could be right. I know I'm right. So, then there's me. Natural rodent control. Timmy here . . ." He lays his hand on the little dog's rump. Timmy jumps up and goes racing half-sideways across the floor, his nails ticking on the bare wood, out of the light of the lamp and into the shadows. There's a snap, a little scream, and a growl. Then Timmy comes back with this rat in his teeth.

Willy Dink takes it from him, holds it up to peer at it, tosses it into a sack, and then pats Timmy on the head. "Good boy," he says, proud as can be. "What do you think of that?"

"I think Timmy's a good boy," I says.

"And fast."

"How about the ferret?"

"Like lightning. But I mostly use him in the walls and under the floors. That's where he works best."

"How about the snake?"

"I use him for the tightest places. Down drains, things like that. This place I'm just sweeping through a couple of times there's so many. I'll get down to the fine work in a couple days when I got most of the bold ones bagged."

We sit there in silence for a minute listening to the city waking up. I realize the time and scramble to my feet.

"My wife'll be having a fit," I says. "I told her I'd be a couple hours."

Willy Dink stands up beside me. I look down into his grimy face which reminds me of drawings of leprechauns I seen in picture books. He comes up to about my shoulder which, since I'm not a tall man, don't happen very often.

"You say your name's Flannery?" he says.

That's what I'd said when we'd introduced each other after Willy Dink had give me the fright.

"You the Flannery what found Baby the gorilla a bedroom over to the steam room in the Paradise Baths?"

I nod my head.

"I done some work for them two, Shimmy Dugan and Princess Grace, what owns the Paradise," Willy Dink says. "You got to be the same Jimmy Flannery, then, what found that body chewed in half by the alligators down in the sewers by the river."

"I try to keep a low profile," I says.

"Oh, sure. Me too. I been down in them sewers."

"How's that?"

"Plenty of rats. Sometimes I catch some live to train my ferrets and dogs and feed my snakes."

"Oh." I got a picture of Willy Dink roaming through the sewers underneath the city with his yellow eyes and pointy nose.

"Seeing as how we're practically friends," he says, "you could do me a favor."

"What's that?"

"You could get the Board of Health, the animal-control officer, and the Business Licensing Bureau off my neck."

"Are they all on your neck?"

"Them and a couple of others what want to spar a couple rounds with me every now and then."

"What's the beef?"

"Keeping a zoo in a dwelling. Trapping exotic pets. Running an animal-husbandry farm without a permit. I can give you the numbers of the ordinances if you want?"

"Well, just let me ask around the different offices first to see if there's anything I can do."

"You scratch my back and I'll scratch yours," he says. "That's how it goes, ain't it?"

"You'll excuse me for asking, and it don't have anything to do with me helping you or not helping you, but how do you think you can scratch my back?"

His eyes open up very wide as though I'm acting pretty dumb. "What do you mean, how can I scratch your back? Anytime you get some vermin in your house I'll come and get them out for free. Also, you want to get into that apartment on the fifth? I can get you into that apartment on the fifth."

8

When we get to Lombardi's orange door, Willy Dink hands me a key.

"Where'd you get the key?" I says in a whisper.

He puts a finger up to his lips and makes with his head that I should shut up and open the door. I do like he says and we're inside. Willy Dink closes the door behind us without making a sound.

When we're inside I says, "Lombardi give you this key?"

He gives me a look like what am I, crazy.

"Kropotkin give it to you?" I says.

He don't change the look. "I got to do my job when I got to do my job. When I'm in hot pursuit, I ain't got time to get permission from somebody who ain't home or get a key from somebody who ain't there. You understand what I'm saying?"

"You could get busted for a B and E."

"They got to catch me in the act. If I don't want to get caught in the act, it's very hard to catch me in the act."

I hand him back the key but he waves it away. "I got another. I always make extras. What are you looking for?"

"I don't know."

"If it's that lady's body, it's not here."

"How do you know?"

"Timmy and me cornered a rat in here last night."

"You just waltzed right in?"

"I don't waltz in if anybody's home. I knock on the door. But she wasn't home."

"How could you be sure of that?"

"Because I saw her leave earlier in the evening with her suitcase."

"So, she could've come back for something she forgot," I says.

"She could've but she didn't."

We've been whispering in the dark for a couple of minutes. I think it's time to turn on the lights. I find the switch next to the door. I hesitate a second before flicking it.

"Go ahead," Willy Dink says in a regular tone of voice. "The drapes is closed."

"Keep it down, will you?" I says, and flick the light.

"The corridor walls is six inches thick. You don't got to worry," Willy Dink says.

Joyce Lombardi's apartment ain't as empty as Kropotkin's but it ain't as full and fancy as Mrs. Warren's. It's balanced in a nice place in between. Lots of waxed pine furniture in the kitchen, wheat-colored fabrics and big pillows in the living room, more pine in the dining area, and just a few unfinished chests and futons on the polished floor in the bedroom.

It's all so neat that, except for a couple of dishes drying in a wooden rack on the sink and a used glass sitting on the coffee table, you'd think nobody was living in the place very much. Like it was a hotel room waiting for somebody to occupy it. Not much to give me a clue to Joyce's personality.

The pictures on the walls are framed prints you can buy anywhere, except for a pink nude in the bedroom over the bed. There's a picture of a girl in a silver frame on the dresser.

"Is this Joyce Lombardi?" I says.

"That's her," Willy Dink says. "Ain't she something?"

It's the face of the blond on top of the pile in Miller's studio.

The connecting bath's a mess. I don't mean there's signs of a struggle. I mean it's the kind of mess what proves that somebody's living there. She caps the toothpaste but don't cap the shampoo. There's a cake of soap melting in the soap dish. The mirror's dotted with spatters from brushing her wet hair.

I open up the medicine cabinet. It's half-empty. There's a used toothbrush but no extra in its plastic box. I don't see any of the little things like blunt-nosed scissors, or tweezers, or a packet of Q-Tips. It looks like the medicine chest of somebody who's gone through it filling up a traveling case.

I open the linen closet and the three drawers next to the sink one by one. Plenty of towels, washcloths, and two bath mats. Two robes made out of turkish toweling and a few packets of those thin cloth slippers the fancier airlines give out on international flights. I guess they're for guests to use after a bath or a shower.

The top drawer's full of things like hand mirrors and shower caps. There's no hair dryer. So, maybe she did come back for it. Maybe she wasn't snatched off the streets on the way home.

There's no sign of blood in the grouting between the tiles on the floor or walls. No sign of it when I wipe my finger around the drains.

I go back into the living room. Willy Dink's sitting on the hearth of the imitation fireplace with his animals on and around him.

"You missed that room," he says, pointing to another door.

"I was just going to have a look," I says.

It's supposed to be the guest bedroom. There's no furniture in it except two stools, a short one and a tall one. A cream enamel industrial lamp hangs down from the ceiling. Every wall that don't have a door or window in it is lined with bookshelves made out of planks and bricks and they're full of books.

The bathroom next to it is very small. Just a toilet, hand basin, and shower stall. There's courtesy packages of things like soap, shampoo, disposable razors, and toothpaste in the cabinet.

I go back and look at the titles on the spines of the books. There's books on every subject you could imagine.

Out in the living room again, I stand in the middle of the floor wondering what's missing.

"No television," I says.

"That ain't natural," Willy Dink says.

There's a low table against the wall and a *TV Guide* on the coffee table alongside the used glass, so it looks like there should be a television set around, but there ain't.

"Maybe it was on the kibosh," Willy Dink says. "Maybe she sent it out to get it fixed."

"Or maybe some doper busts in to heist the price of a fix and she walks in on him. He panics and hits her. Maybe breaks her neck."

"Wouldn't she give him a fight?" Willy Dink says. "I don't see no sign of no fight."

"There ain't much in this room could get knocked over," I says. "It could have happened that way, couldn't it, Willy?"

He's looking all around the room with his pointy nose sniffing out the corners and his little yellow eyes looking for things nobody but him, the ferret, and the snake could probably see.

"Or she could have surprised somebody she knew prowling around in here. Maybe she starts giving him hell. Threatens she's going to get Kropotkin over. Maybe he grabs her to shut her up and kills her without meaning to kill her. So he hides the body and steals the television set so it'll *look* like there was a thief," I says.

"That somebody could've been Kropotkin hisself," Willy

Dink says, his head still swinging back and forth, trying to catch a hint from the air in the room. All of a sudden his head stops shifting and he stares at me and sees me staring at him.

"Oh, no," he says. "Don't stick the tail on me."

"How come you're so sure she didn't come back last night?"

"Because I would've heard her. I would've heard the elevator."

"And you never heard the elevator?"

"I wish I could say I did."

"How about the stairs?"

"It's possible I could miss that."

"But you don't really think so."

"I could miss somebody using the stairs if I was busy with a rat or listening to the walls."

"Much traffic in this building after dark?"

"Kropotkin hardly ever goes out then. The lady on the third floor, never. The other tenant on the fifth is gone. The workers in the zipper factory are gone by five."

"How about the photographer on the second floor?"

"He comes and goes."

"How about yesterday?"

"He left for the day the first time about four o'clock."

"The first time?"

"Well, he was in and out all day. But he usually leaves around four, five, most days, unless he goes out for something to eat, and then he comes back in about an hour and sometimes stays overnight."

"So last night?"

"Went out at about four, back at five, out again about half an hour later. Then he come back again, must have been six-thirty. I was outside and saw his lights go on."

"So he stayed overnight?"

"No. He left again around midnight. That was the last time."

I stare at the wall, wondering should I mention that what he just told me is exactly the sort of thing he'd tell me if he was the one Joyce Lombardi caught prowling around her apartment after he'd used his key to get in. When I turn around to look for Willy Dink, he ain't there.

Now I hear what he heard before I heard it, the opening of the front door.

"Don't move," Kropotkin says, standing there with his little ax. "I think I caught me a burglar."

9

I do some of the best talking of my life. I dazzle Kropotkin with footwork. I duck, I dodge, I give him ripple-dipple and ropa-dope. I'm a wonder if I do say so myself. All the time I'm doing this performance my knees are shaking and I got a bladder that all of a sudden feels like it's going to bust. Looking at Kropotkin in his underwear, holding that ax ready to chop me down the middle, is enough to loosen a sphincter muscle or two.

Finally he takes mercy on me when I tell him how bad I got to use the convenience.

"Well, all right," he says. "Go wring out your sock."

I knock-knee it to Joyce Lombardi's toilet.

"When you're through," Kropotkin says, "make sure you flush it. And don't piss on her floor. And put the seat down, for God's sake."

I do everything like he says. When I come out drying my hands on my handkerchief he says, "Tell me again how come you're breaking and entering."

"I couldn't sleep. I kept wondering how come this young lady packs some stuff in her suitcase and goes across town to move in with this friend of mine. Drops the suitcase in the middle of the floor. Don't even start unpacking. Turns on the tape deck. Why does she do that she's in such a hurry to leave?"

"I always put the music on first thing I come into the house. I don't like to be alone in a quiet house. You know what I mean?"

"I know what you mean. So, okay, that part, she turns on the music for some company, I understand. I'll give you that. So what does she do next?"

"She goes makes herself a drink, a cup of coffee, a glass of tea. If she knows the kitchen good enough. If she's got permission."

"Oh, she's got permission."

"So did you ask this Canarias woman was there a used glass or a coffee cup on a table? On the kitchen counter?"

I'm feeling better. Kropotkin's treating me like a partner in trying to work this thing through instead of like a burglar he'll maybe smack with his little ax. Which, thank God, he's tucked under his armpit.

"I didn't ask."

"You should've asked."

"I can see that."

"Let's go over to my place," he says.

"Can I use your phone?"

"Sure. I'll make you a glass of tea while you make your call. It's a local?"

"I want to call my wife. I told her I'd be back in a couple hours. Now look at the time."

"Time flies when you're having fun, don't it?" Kropotkin says, patting the handle of the ax and grinning at his own joke.

When I get Mary on the phone she says, "Five more minutes and I'd be late leaving for work."

"I'm really very sorry," I says.

"I had pictures of that giant Kropotkin catching you and chopping you up with his little ax," Mary says. "Like that nursery rhyme, 'Fee, fie, fo, fum, I smell the blood of an Irishman.' "

"That's an 'Englishman,' " I says.

"Who gives a rat's ass?" Mary says which, since she hardly ever uses a word like that, I know she's mad even though she's trying not to show it.

"Well, that's what happened," I says.

"What's what happened?"

"Rats. I met up with Willy Dink, this rat catcher. I sit on the floor of an empty loft sharing Willy Dink's coffee and buns while his ferret, his king snake, and his terrier run around killing rats."

"Spectator sports," she says.

"What's that supposed to mean?"

"How can a woman expect a man to call her up and tell her everything's all right and he's not dead when he's watching a spectator sport?"

It always amazes me how women can get from here to Pittsburgh by way of New Orleans. It's a talent they have.

"Who says watching a snake swallow a rat is a sport? Who says I could've reached out and got my hand on a telephone? Who says, most of all, that anybody's been murdered?"

"Isn't that what we've been talking about since Janet came to ask for your help?" she says.

"What I think is she gets a call from the boyfriend. They make it up and go off for a weekend like to Atlantic City."

"I remember Atlantic City," she says.

"I got to hang up," I says. "I'm tying up this person's phone."

"What person?"

"Kropotkin."

"Oh, my God."

"It's all right. He invited me in for a glass of tea."

"Watch he doesn't put rat poison in it."

"That's Willy Dink you got to watch out for that."

After she tells me twice to call her again as soon as I get back home, I hang up and sit down to have a glass of tea with Kropotkin. Like we was old friends. Partners.

"You'll be seeing cops tomorrow morning. I'm surprised they ain't been around already," I says.

"How's that? It ain't been even forty-eight yet."

"Alderman Canarias asks a favor."

"Alderman? That woman what came knocking on my door asking me to let her in is an alderman?"

"That's right."

"Interesting."

"In what way interesting?"

"I've been trying to get this here building put on the historic-buildings register. It was built about the same time as the Rullin mansion down the street. You know, that three-story brick where they got that funny museum."

"What funny museum is that?"

"They show photographs what jump out of the wall at you."

"Holograms?"

"Whatever. Anyway. This factory was built by old Jacob Rullin back in the eighties, so I figure it should be on the registry just like the house he lived in."

"Well, I suppose that'd be nice," I says.

"More than nice. I could get some tax benefits. Maybe even a restoration grant. You see what I mean?"

"I see that you're thinking how nice it'd be if we found Joyce Lombardi for Alderman Canarias. You're thinking how grateful she'd be and how happy she'd be to do Kropotkin a favor."

"I like the way your mind works, Flannery. So, you want to go back into Joyce's flat? You want to go anywheres else?"

"I'd like to go into Scanlan's."

He hesitates for only a minute, pictures of city-hall patronage dancing in his head. He heaves himself up and grunts, "You got it." He picks up a key off the rack on the wall.

"All the tenants give me one in case of fire."

I nod my head, thinking that Kropotkin having a key to every corner of the building is something to think about. For a security building there's an awful lot of people who seem to be able to go anywhere they want and plenty of ways in for somebody who ain't even got any keys.

Kropotkin opens the door to Scanlan's. It's gloomy inside because the blinds are down and the drapes are closed.

"This is the smallest flat," Kropotkin says.

I can see that. It's nice but there's nothing grand about it. It looks like the kind of place a bachelor who ain't in it except once in a while would have. Plain furniture bought in a bunch. Wall-to-wall carpet. A Formica dinette set over by the kitchen.

None of the lamps are on. I go around looking to see if one of them is plugged into a timer. They're not.

I check out the kitchen. There's nothing in the refrigerator except some canned sodas. Nothing that could go bad while somebody was away for a couple of weeks or a month. There's a glass on the pass-through counter with a little whiskey and water in the bottom.

"What are you looking for?" Kropotkin says again.

I walk over to the bedroom door and put my hand on the knob. "Like you said. Somebody's waiting for somebody in an empty house, they maybe make themselves a cup of coffee or some tea."

I'm looking at Kropotkin while I'm saying this. He's staring past me over my shoulder into Scanlan's bedroom. He's white as a sheet.

I turn around quick. A naked woman's laying on the bed with her legs spread, her head turned to one side, and her eyes staring at the window. There's a fat, bright orange plastic tube cradled up against her neck. There's a sparkling earring on the ear I can see.

"Joyce Lombardi?" I says.

10

I call the cops. I call Captain Dominick Pescaro direct.

"You know this Joyce Lombardi Alderman Canarias asks you to do a favor go look for her?" I says.

"We're looking."

"How hard are you looking?"

"If you're going to start one of them tunes about police cover-up, I'm going to send Rourke and O'Shea out looking for you and when they find you they'll break your arms and legs."

"I don't know about cover-up. How about nonfeasance?"

"You shouldn't use words you don't understand," he says. "You're the cross God gave me to bear, Flannery. I know that. But do me a favor. Inspect the sewers. Knock on doors and get votes. Stay home with your wife and start a family."

"I called to say you don't have to look anymore."

"She showed up?"

"She showed up dead."

"Where are you?" he says, his voice losing the drawl it gets when he trades insults with me. Now it's clipped and sharp like scissors snapping open and shut.

I give him the address.

"Five minutes," he says.

While we're waiting I put in a call to Mary over to Passavant.

"I found Janet's friend," I says.

"How bad?" she says, reading my voice.

"As bad as it gets."

She don't say anything for a minute. She sees more death and tragedy in a day that I see in a month.

"Where are you?" she finally asks.

"I'm in this apartment in the building where Joyce lived."

"She's not in her own apartment?"

"She's in this other apartment," I says. "I'll explain when I get out of here."

"How long will that be?"

"I don't know. I just called the cops. Could be an hour. Could be more."

"Have you called Janet?"

"I didn't do that because I didn't think it would be such a good idea to break the news to her over the telephone. Especially when she was down there at her office all by herself."

"I'll get somebody to cover for me and I'll go over there and tell her."

"You don't have to do that you don't want to," I says. "I can do it after I finish up with the cops."

"I'll do it."

"Well, I've had experience delivering bad news," I says.

"I have too, James. I've had plenty."

"But this is a friend."

"I've had to break the hearts of friends before. I'll see if I can get her to come to our place with me."

"See if you can find my old man," I says. "Get him over too."

"Like family," Mary says.

"Well, she's got nobody else and it's always better to have too many people around what love you than too few. Mike makes her laugh and it'll help, after the shock wears off, she should laugh a little."

"We'll be at home."

"I'll get there as soon as I can," I says.

I hang up. Kropotkin and me sit there in Scanlan's living room with the door open listening for the elevator.

"I wonder where Willy Dink's got to?" I says.

"Back in his hole, wherever that is. Taking a sleep somewhere in the walls. Who knows? The man sleeps by day and lives by night."

The elevator rumbles up the five floors. The door slides open. I hear these feet pounding nails into the linoleum in the hallway, the way cops walk.

In thirty seconds Francis O'Shea and Murray Rourke, fat and skinny, rough and smooth, tough and tender, are standing in the doorway looking Kropotkin and me over like they expect to see signs of cannibalism.

"You know, Flannery, I'm going to hire you out to my brother-in-law, Jackie Diversey," O'Shea says, rubbing his nose which is like a red pickle. "He tells me his undertaking business is a little slow and I never see a man collect dead bodies the way you do."

"I don't think it's funny a young woman's dead," I says.

"My God, butter wouldn't melt in your mouth, Flannery," O'Shea says as he walks past me toward the open door to the bedroom.

Rourke follows him, throwing a glance and a smile at me and saying, "How you doing, Jimmy? Was the door to the bedroom open when you came in?"

"No. I opened it."

"How come you opened it?" O'Shea says from the doorway.

"I was looking around."

"You was looking around by yourself or you was looking around with this person here?"

"My name is Hyman Kropotkin. I'm the owner of this building. Also I live down the hall," Kropotkin says, hot under the collar.

Rourke smiles and lifts up his hand with the palm out.

"No need to get upset, Mr. Kropotkin. We just want to know who's who and what's what. Where's the tenant lives in this apartment?"

"He's out of town."

"Well, see, like that. How come you're in this apartment when the tenant isn't at home? That could be breaking and entering."

"I got a key. I got permission," Kropotkin says.

The elevator starts to rumble going down.

O'Shea's all the way into the bedroom. He's standing by the bed looking down at the woman. Rourke has reached the doorway. Kropotkin's standing next to him. I'm still in the middle of the living room.

"You got the tenant's permission to go waltzing through his house when he's out?" Rourke says, in this pleasant way he's got that calls you a liar.

"I asked him to let me in," I says.

"How come is that, Jimmy?"

"Because I was looking for Joyce Lombardi."

"This Joyce Lombardi?" O'Shea sings out from beside the bed.

Kropotkin, who'd had a close look right after we found her, nods his head.

"The landlord says that's who it is," Rourke says.

"I didn't hear him."

"He's nodding his head."

The elevator's coming up.

Rourke steps out of the doorway to let O'Shea come back out.

"So you took a gander at the naked lady?" O'Shea says, making it sound nasty.

"Well, I had to see who was laying on Mr. Scanlan's bed, didn't I?" Kropotkin says.

"You had to see too, did you, Flannery?"

"I had to see was she dead."

"You satisfied yourself about that?"

"I had a close look."

"You have anything else? Like maybe a little feel?"

"For God's sake, Francis," Rourke says.

"Have a little decency," I says.

"There's a naked corpse in there with her legs wide open," O'Shea says, waving his thumb over his shoulder, turning red in the face, "and you two are getting delicate."

"It's what you're suggesting turns my stomach," Rourke says.

O'Shea spins around on his partner and says, "For Christ's sake, we know about worse than some crazy having it off with a dead body."

"You're talking to Jimmy Flannery," Rourke says. "Show a little sense, Francis."

Captain Pescaro comes walking through the door. "What's going on here?"

"Your detective here's got a filthy mind," Kropotkin says.

"Who're you?" Pescaro says, stepping up close to Kropotkin, standing toe to toe, staring him down even though he's got to bend his head back and look up. It's hard to intimidate a giant like Kropotkin by invading his space, but Pescaro makes it work.

Kropotkin mumbles who he is and backs off two feet.

Pescaro goes to the bedroom door. "You got an identification?"

"It's Joyce Lombardi," I says.

"How come you found her, Flannery?"

"We were just getting Flannery's testimony on that, Captain," O'Shea says.

"So?"

Janet Canarias comes over to my place and asks me can I ask around about this friend of hers."

"That much I figured out by myself."

"I was over talking to Mr. Kropotkin last night. He ain't seen her since the day before. He told me a couple of people besides Janet Canarias, a man and a woman, was knocking on her door all day yesterday."

"Was the man her neighbor? The one who lives here?"

"No, the one who came around more than once was a stranger to Mr. Kropotkin. The man who lives in this apartment's a salesman and he's out on the road. That's all Mr. Kropotkin can tell me. When I walk down the elevator I pass this front door and I see light under it once. Later on I walk past and it's out. I figure it's on a timer to discourage thieves. When I get home I talk it over with Mary."

"How's Mary?" Rourke says.

O'Shea throws his partner a dirty look for interrupting my "testimony" that way. "Go on," he says.

"I wondered would somebody worry about timers in what's supposed to be a security building," I says.

"*Supposed* to be?" Kropotkin says, like I stepped on his toe.

"I got to tell you, Mr. Kropotkin, there's a lot of ways to get into this building and these apartments when you look around a little," I says. "Anyway, now it looks like maybe the killer was in here while we was chewing the fat."

He don't say anything about how maybe Willy Dink was my way in here and there, and neither do I. Don't ask me why Kropotkin don't blow the whistle on Willy Dink. My reason is that I don't want O'Shea and Pescaro yelling in his face after the little man did me the favor and let me into Joyce's flat. At least, not yet.

"Never mind all that," Pescaro says. "Just tell me why you got up out of your nice warm bed to come prowling around a building on Morgan."

"I couldn't sleep. I'm laying there in bed thinking that Joyce Lombardi arrives over to Janet Canarias' apartment around four o'clock in the afternoon, sets down her suitcase, turns on the tape deck, and then leaves. How come she leaves? Because she forgot something at her apartment here and comes back to get it?"

"What?" O'Shea says. "What does she come back for?"

"There's no hair dryer in her suitcase. Maybe she came back for that. Maybe that's her hair dryer around her neck."

11

Fifteen minutes later we got a crowd. The boys from Forensics has arrived. They got me and Kropotkin crowded into the kitchen with O'Shea and Rourke after they do what they do to the counters and the cabinets and the glass on the counter. Pescaro's in the bedroom watching them take pictures, making sure they do the coverage.

When he comes into the kitchen I ask him does the medical examiner know what killed her.

"Strangled with the cord of that hair dryer." He gives me a long, hard look. "What the hell's everybody doing crowded in the kitchen? Is this a goddamn wake? Somebody pouring drinks?"

"Forensics told us to stay out of the way."

Pescaro sticks his head out of the kitchen door. "Hey! You through in the living room?"

"You can go in and sit you want to, but don't touch anything on the tables," somebody yells back.

"So, okay," Pescaro says, "let's go take a load off our feet."

We all go into the living room and sit down. I feel like I'm in the smoking room of a funeral home except nobody's smoking. The three cops are sitting there staring at their feet.

"No clothes," Pescaro says.

"What?" Kropotkin says as though he thinks the remark is directed exclusively at him.

"There's no sign of any female garments in this apartment. Nowhere. If she came in here for a little . . ."

"She's got her own place down the hall," I says.

The elevator starts making a racket again. It's like thunder coming up from the river.

"Even if she was dragged in here," O'Shea says, "her clothes should be here somewheres."

"So, what does that tell you?" Pescaro says.

"Her clothes is somewheres else?" I says.

"That's right. And if her clothes are somewhere else, chances are she was killed somewhere else."

O'Shea and Rourke look at one another, then at their boss.

"Call for some uniforms," Pescaro says. "As many as you need. Do this place like there's gold dust in the floor cracks. Anybody you find at home make a list and tell them to stay there. Tell them we'll be coming to talk to them."

Harold Boardman from Forensics comes out. He's wearing throwaway gloves that make his hands look clumsy and deformed. He's carrying the hair dryer in a plastic bag.

"Finished here," he says.

"Is there one of them missing from the bathroom?" Pescaro says.

"If there was one missing from the bathroom how would I know if there was one missing from the bathroom?" Boardman says.

"You find one?"

"We don't find one."

"So, okay, she was maybe in the bathroom and this gamoosh comes on with her. She resists and he grabs the closest thing he can get his hands on."

"What was she doing naked in a man's bathroom she should resist when he lays a hand on her?" I says.

I hear the tap-tap-tap of a woman in heels walking fast and the squeak of rubber soles. I turn to the door just as Janet and Mary come through. Mary throws a look at me that says there was nothing she could do to keep Janet from coming. Janet looks around, swinging her head right and left like a frightened animal looking for a way out. Then she heads for the open bedroom door.

Rourke reaches out a hand, but she tilts herself around it. Pescaro tells her not to go into the room, but she ignores him. I start to chase after her, but Mary stops me and says, "Let her look, if she's got to look."

Janet stops in the doorway for a second. She plants her feet as though afraid she's going to fall. Then she takes a step and lets out a yell. Harold Boardman, this youngster from Forensics, sees her heading for the body and manages to do what none of the rest of us could do. He steps between her and the bed and throws his arms around her. For a second she tries to fight past him, but he holds on and turns her around because he knows she really wants to be turned around now that she's seen what she was afraid to see.

"Won't somebody close her eyes?" she says. "Won't somebody cover her with something?"

By the time he's walked her to a chair and sat her down, she's got hold of herself. She's quiet the way people are quiet after they've checked for themselves that the messenger bringing the bad news wasn't mistaken. She pulls her hair back from her temples with both hands and looks up at me.

I kneel down beside her chair and take her hand. "I'm sorry."

"You found her," she says.

I don't know what to say.

"Now I want you to promise me you'll find the one who did it."

I don't give her the song and dance about how it's up to the cops now. I glance up at Pescaro. He nods his head, giving me permission.

"I'll do what I can, Janet. I'll start on it right away. Now, will you go home with Mary and I'll see you later on."

Mary comes over and we help Janet to her feet, which she lets us do although she's got herself under control.

We turn to the front door. A man in a suede jacket and a Tyrolean hat is standing in the doorway with a sample case in his hand. "Just what the hell is going on here?" he says.

"Who're you?" Pescaro says.

"I'm the man who lives here," he says. "I'm William Scanlan."

12

Forensics is gone. It's Pescaro, O'Shea, Rourke, Scanlan and, by the grace of the silent promise he makes to Canarias when Pescaro nods to me, myself sitting in Scanlan's living room.

The salesman's sitting down, still wearing his hat. He's a mouth breather and every time he lets it out the smell of whiskey hits me.

"Ain't you warm in that thing, Mr. Scanlan?" Rourke says.

"What?" Scanlan says, looking at Rourke with eyes like a couple of hard-boiled eggs. A thousand little veins are busted across his cheeks and nose. His jowls are white and pasty. Even so, it's pretty plain that he was a good-looking man once upon a time.

"Your hat. You should take it off," O'Shea says. "You're sweating. You go out again and you'll get a chill."

"Go out?" Scanlan says, standing up and taking off his hat. "Why should I go out?" He rubs his hand over his bald scalp, then smooths down his fringe of hair all around.

"Maybe to get something out of your car," Pescaro says.

"That's right," Rourke chimes in, "maybe there's something you need that you left in your car?"

"Like maybe you left your telephone book in the glove compartment," O'Shea says.

"I got my telephone book. I got one here in my pocket and I got another one over there by the phone."

"We looked through that one, Mr. Scanlan," Pescaro says. "You don't mind we took a look?"

"I don't mind. Why should I mind?"

"Well, that's hard to say. We don't read minds, Mr. Scanlan, do we?" Rourke says in his sweet way.

They're working him and Scanlan's been around long enough to know they're working him and it's scaring him a lot. They fall into a pattern, taking turns, Pescaro to Rourke to O'Shea. Doing triple plays on him. Making him turn his head from one to the other, breaking his concentration.

Pescaro starts. "We see you got a lot of ladyfriends."

Scanlan tries to make hisself a roguish grin but it comes out all crooked like it's made of melting wax. "I got a few. You know how it is. Salesman on the road."

"Gets very lonely."

"That's right. All those motel rooms. Hotel rooms."

"How many would you say you know?"

"How many what? Motels? Hotels?"

"We're trying to make ourselves clear, Mr. Scanlan," Pescaro says. "You know we don't mean hotels. How many ladyfriends have you got? Is every woman's name in your telephone book a ladyfriend?"

"Well, no, some of them are buyers. Plenty of them are buyers and shopkeepers. I'm in costume jewelry. You know?"

"No, we don't. We don't know about jewelry. Except it's stolen. We're cops."

"I was just saying that most of the women's names in the book are business contacts."

"Not ladyfriends?"

"Well, friends, but not how you mean ladyfriends."

"How do you think Detective O'Shea means ladyfriends?" Pescaro says.

"Well, you know."

"Like Joyce Lombardi?"

"She was a neighbor."

"Her number's in your book. What do you need a neighbor's number she lives forty feet down the hall?"

"Sometimes when I'm on the road I'd give her a call."

"Why would you do that?" Pescaro says.

"Ask her if anybody was coming around asking for me."

"Why would anybody do that?"

"Well, you know, friends."

"Don't your friends know you're a traveling salesman? Don't they know you go away for weeks at a time?"

"Sure, but . . ."

"So why would you call Joyce Lombardi?" Pescaro asks again.

"Sometimes I'd ask her to do a little favor."

"What kind of favor?"

"Well, you know."

"Goddammit, Scanlan," O'Shea explodes, "we don't know. If we knew we wouldn't be asking. What goddammit kind of favor?"

"I got men buyers too. Sometimes they come to town on a business trip they're lonely."

"Just like you get lonely out in those hotel and motel rooms?" O'Shea says, breaking the pattern, moving in on Scanlan with the hammer.

"That's right. They ask me can I arrange for them to have a companion. Some nice girl they can take to dinner. Talk to."

"About the wife and kiddies?"

"Yeah, like that."

"So you do these favors for these buyers even when you ain't in town. Lombardi does these favors for you because you're neighbors?"

"Well, she gets something out of the dates. She's a young woman on her own. How much money can she make being a model? This ain't New York. She's no headliner."

"Just a pretty girl," Pescaro says. "So what does she get out of these dates?"

"Well, she gets a good meal and a night out."

"And maybe these lonely buyers are grateful and give her some money for the rent?"

"She works them for the rent I don't know anything about it. That's up to her and whoever she's out with."

"Suppose this buyer or that buyer don't give her a little something toward the rent," O'Shea says, his voice going soft, working the pedals, playing the music to go with the words.

"What do you mean?"

"I mean do you give her a little something for her time and trouble?"

"Well, I could do. Just to help her out."

"So now we know, don't we?"

"Know what?"

"You're a pimp, Mr. Scanlan," O'Shea says.

Scanlan's face crumples up like he's about to cry. "For God's sake, it wasn't like that. All I was trying to do was help her out with her expenses. And do some favors for some business acquaintances."

"You buy any favors for yourself?" O'Shea said, putting a nasty twist on it.

"I took Joyce out for dinner a few times, but it wasn't nothing like that."

"Like what?" Rourke says.

"She wasn't a hooker and I wasn't a john."

"But you slept together."

"No, we never did."

"You telling me you didn't hit on a beautiful girl like that?"

"I wanted to, but she didn't want to."

Pescaro stands up like he needs to stretch his legs. "So,

maybe you're not a pimp, Mr. Scanlan, maybe you're only a procurer."

After that sinks in Rourke bends forward in his chair a little. "Tell us, Mr. Scanlan," he says, and Scanlan leans forward too, toward the quiet, sweet-spoken cop. He's ready to fall into Rourke's arms and cooperate. "Tell us, did you call Miss Lombardi this trip—like the day before yesterday—and ask her would she like to go out on a date with one of your acquaintances?"

"No. God as my witness. No."

"Too bad," O'Shea says.

Scanlan jerks his head around. "Why do you say that?"

"Well, if you'd sent Miss Lombardi out on a date, we'd have good reason to look elsewhere for whoever murdered her."

Scanlan was staring at O'Shea with his mouth hanging open, hearing O'Shea's next remark without him even having to say it.

"Now we got to keep looking closer to home," O'Shea said.

"I wasn't even in town," Scanlan said, his voice getting thin. "I can prove I was somewhere else."

"Where else?"

"Wherever I was whenever you say Joyce got herself killed."

"Hell, Mr. Scanlan, nowadays? You heard of airplanes? They come and they go. Man can pop in and out of towns here, there and everywhere like a goddamn Mexican jumping bean," O'Shea said, grinning happily. "Buy a commuter ticket with any name he likes. Who's to know?"

"You want to tell us anything?" Rourke says.

I get up and walk over to the corner of the room. Pescaro gets my drift and joins me.

"What is it, Flannery?" Pescaro says.

"Shouldn't you be reading this poor sucker his rights?"

"We're not charging him yet, Flannery. We're not arresting him."

"You're screwing a confession out of him."

"Well, that's what you say. That's not what I say. We're just asking a few questions, trying to clear up this tragedy."

"Ain't you afraid the court will rule that you've poisoned the well?"

"You're not a lawyer, Flannery. Don't try to talk like a lawyer to me. I got to tell you. In the latest rulings, honest police error in procedure don't taint the evidence or a confession."

"You still should read that poor bastard his rights."

"When I'm ready to put the cuffs on him, he'll get read his rights. You open your mouth and I'll kick your ass out of here. You're in here on a pass."

"How come you're so generous to me?"

"Because I don't want you or that Canarias woman yelling police corruption. That's your favorite tune."

"I ain't the only one singing it."

"You just mind your manners. Remember. You're just a fly on the wall. I don't want to hear a peep."

When we go back to the others, Rourke is practically chatting with Scanlan like they're old buddies chewing the fat over a glass of beer. He's waiting for his boss to get back into it before going for Scanlan's throat again.

"Nobody's accusing you of anything, Mr. Scanlan," Pescaro says. "I want you to understand that."

"Well, I'm certainly glad to hear that," Scanlan says in this hearty way like he's just been told a buyer wants to buy of ton of colored stones and tin.

"You sure there's nothing in your car you'd like to get?"

"No, I got everything."

"But you don't have your suitcase, do you?"

Scanlan looks around the floor at his feet as though a

suitcase is like a dog that'll come to him when he calls. "I guess not," he says.

"So, why don't you let us go down and get it for you? Dirty clothes left in a suitcase start to smell."

So, now I know they got something to push in his face that I don't know about.

Scanlan turns white.

"Dirty clothes left in a bathroom hamper does the same thing," Pescaro says. "So, why don't you just go down with Rourke and O'Shea and get your suitcase out of your car?"

I'm about to tell Scanlan that he's got rights and they haven't got a warrant to search his car. Pescaro stares at me and I shut up. It probably don't matter anyway because if the suitcase in the car is empty they'll connect it back to the dirty clothes in the hamper and that could give them probable cause for searching the car.

Scanlan gets up like a man walking in his sleep and goes out with the two detectives.

"When they come back, I'll read Scanlan his rights," Pescaro says.

13

When I get back to my own flat my father's there alone.

"Where's Mary and Janet?" I says.

"When the coroner's office called to say they were finished with the postmortem . . ."

"What? The crowds they get down there, how could they be through with a body they got a few hours ago?"

"Politics is a wonderful thing, Jimmy, my boy. Primary time is near and you can bet the mayor's people won't miss a bet keeping an independent alderman sweet. They put that poor girl at the head of the list."

I call the morgue and ask for Harold Boardman, the youngster who stopped Janet from getting to Joyce. I tell him who I am and ask him to do me the favor, tell me what they found out.

"Death by strangulation. Got her from behind and put a knee in her back. There's a bruise."

"Was she raped?"

"Technically, no. Legally, yes."

"How's that?"

"There was neither ejaculation nor penetration, but there was evidence of an attempt to have intercourse."

"Her family come to claim her?"

"As far as we know she had no next of kin. Alderman Canarias has volunteered to arrange for burial and take the expense off the city's hands."

"I owe you one," I says.

"I'll remember," he says.

I hang up. Mike's looking at me.

"Janet's going to bury her," I says.

He nods. "I hear that Pescaro's letting you sit in on the investigation into who killed her."

"Sit in on what? They got the man."

"Well, that was quick," Mike says, very much surprised. Being a fireman all his life, he hasn't got a very high opinion of the Chicago Police's ability to solve important cases. "So, tell me."

He sits down with his mug of coffee while I give him the story of how the cops found some dirty laundry in the clothes hamper and the empty suitcase in Scanlan's car, and how this is evidence that Scanlan comes home once *before* he walked through the door pretending he'd just arrived.

"He says he comes home, takes off his hat and coat, and tosses the suitcase on the couch. Makes hisself a drink in the kitchen. Brings it back and opens his suitcase. It's filled with dirty underwear and socks and he wants to put them in the hamper. Takes a leak. Goes into the bedroom to take off his clothes and get into a robe. There's the naked neighbor laying dead on the bed. He gets dressed in a hurry. Grabs his hat, coat, and suitcase and gets the hell out of there."

"Why didn't he call the police?"

"For God's sake. He says he walks in and finds a naked corpse of a girl who lives in the same building, right down the hall. A person he knows good enough to take out for dinner and, the way everybody's likely to think, good enough to be going to bed with. Somebody he sets up on dates with out-of-town buyers."

"Pimping?"

"He says not pimping. Just doing a couple of favors. Helping Joyce Lombardi out with a good meal and a night on the town. Maybe the date gives her a little present for her time. Who knows for what else? It's none of his business. A girl don't have to lay on her back because she takes a date with an out-of-town buyer. Man don't have to be a pimp he makes a couple of introductions."

"He's a pimp," Mike says, passing final judgment.

"Then Janet's lovelight was a whore."

Mike don't like that idea. "A girl goes out socially, accepts a little financial help, don't make her a prostitute."

"If the date's set up by a man you call a pimp what does it make her if it don't make her a prostitute?"

"It makes her a young woman in a big city struggling to keep body and soul together. You can't go around judging people the way you do, Jimmy."

He's doing it to me again. My father does this thing where he makes an outrageous statement which I dispute and before you know it he's got it twisted around where it's me what said unkind and ungenerous things about somebody and him that's defending their reputations and scolding me for having a mean spirit.

"Wait a second," I says. "I'm not the one called her a whore and him a pimp."

"You've got to show more Christian charity. Remember your dear mother, God bless her soul. She never had an unkind word for anyone and you should take the lesson. Especially you shouldn't speak ill of the dead." He looks at me with his patented bland expression. "So, go on with your story, son. You believe what he said?"

"It could've happened. He could've panicked and run off. Drove off somewhere. He says to a saloon. He wanted time to figure out what the hell he should do. If he reports the body he's going to have everything including his fingernails—"

"And his asshole, even his asshole."

"—examined. He waited awhile, he says. Had a couple three. Thought about putting in an anonymous call from a public booth. Decided to go home and park outside and think some more."

"Sees the action."

"And walked in like he'd just got back in town."

"Only he forgets the dirty socks and don't expect anyone would think of looking into his suitcase."

"That's the way it could've happened."

"It's pretty thin."

"The cops thought so. They arrested him. Pescaro's celebrating right this minute for closing a murder case quicker than anybody in Chicago history."

"That Pescaro's smarter than I thought," Mike says.

I don't say anything. He's looking at me cockeyed.

"It's just as well," he says.

"What's just as well?"

"It's just as well Pescaro cleared this murder up quick. For one thing, you can go back to being a sewer inspector and a precinct captain. What with the mayoral election coming up and all, you got to go banging on doors. You don't have the time for chasing murderers. Besides, now that you're a married man, it's about time you gave up that sort of thing."

"What sort of thing?"

"Well, you know what I mean. You always seem to be stumbling over a corpse."

He makes it sound like I throw them in front of my own feet. I'm ready to say something when the phone rings.

I pick it up. It's my boss and chinaman, Chips Delvin, the old warlord of the Twenty-seventh.

"It's Jimmy Flannery, is it?" he says after I says hello.

"How are you, Mr. Delvin?" I says.

"As well as can be expected, a man my age."

"What can I do for you?" I says.

"We haven't had a chat in some time, have we?"

"And the primary's heating up," I says.

"Well, there's that, but I really want to consult you on another matter altogether. Could you work me into your schedule?"

"I could stop over late this after—"

"I knew you could. How about within the hour? I'll have Mrs. Banjo put the kettle on," he says, paying me no attention, and hangs up in my ear.

"What did old Chips have to say?" Mike asks.

"I think he wants to ask a favor."

14

I go over to Bridgeport, about five miles southwest of the Loop on the South Branch of the Chicago River. What's called the Hamburg section is an old-fashioned neighborhood which probably has more churches and saloons than any other in the city. It's where Hizzoner, the late Richard J. Daley, was born and raised, cutting his political teeth on fistfights and handshaking.

Delvin's house is on a street of houses that look almost alike except for the paint, the pattern of the lace curtains in the windows, and the size of the trees at the curb. Once there was different kinds of furniture on the porches but television did away with that. People don't use their porches the way they used to anymore.

I always get this funny feeling that I'm stepping into my own past when I walk up the steps to Delvin's oak door with the pane of beveled glass set into it. It's like when my old man sings "I'll be down to get you in a taxi, honey" and I get this feeling around my heart like I'm sad for something I once knew but which is gone forever. I wasn't around when they were dancing to that song, so what have I got to feel sad about? Still I get this funny feeling.

I ring the bell and Delvin's housekeeper, Mrs. Banjo, opens the door.

"Are you expected?" she says.

"It's Jimmy Flannery, Mrs. Banjo."

"I can see that, can't I? Do you think I'm getting senile?"

"It's just that every time I come to visit, Mrs. Banjo, you act like you never seen me before and that I wasn't invited."

"This is Mr. Delvin's place of business so to speak," she says. "It's a matter of the dignity of the office."

"Oh, I see," I says, and the funny thing is I do. It's like you can call the archbishop Harry when you're out playing golf with him, but it's Your Grace when you go over to the manse on business. Not that I play golf with the archbishop. I don't play the game at all.

"Well, don't stand there letting the dust in," she says.

I walk past her into the dark hallway where the walls are covered with brown fading photographs of men in bowler hats and women in long skirts.

"You go straight on into the parlor," she says. "You'll have a tea?"

"I'd rather have coffee, if you've got it," I says.

"He's switched to tea. You'll have a cup of tea with a little something warm in it."

I don't argue about putting booze into the tea though she knows by now that I hardly ever touch the stuff. She knows I don't drink it, but Delvin does. He's not supposed to have more than one tot the morning, one the afternoon, and one the evening. He finds ways around that.

Delvin's dozing off in his big, broken-down easy chair, himself a big, broken-down man whose eyes are always weeping like an elephant's. He's got no children and he's almost forgotten the wife that died years ago, so he's like a celibate priest living in a gloomy house with a housekeeper who treats him like he's got the ear of Christ one minute and like a naughty schoolboy the next.

I sit down across from him. The gray light of the overcast day comes through the lace curtains, casting these patterns on his face. I sit there staring at his face, counting the holes of light on top of the wrinkles until he senses someone in the room and snorts hisself awake.

"For God's sake, you walk soft, Jimbo. I can't understand a man who walks so soft. You wonder can he be trusted."

"I tiptoed in," I says.

"How's that?"

"I didn't want to disturb your thoughts."

"I wasn't sleeping," he says.

". . . disturb your thoughts," I says again.

"How's that?"

"I could see you were deep in thought," I says.

"That's right. So I was."

Now that we've got that sorted out, he looks around as though expecting the people in his dreams to come to join us, just as Mrs. Banjo comes in with a tray and the tea things and puts it on a footstool where I can reach them. Two cups arc already poured. When I hand one to Delvin, the smell of the whiskey rises up and pinches my nose. I take the smallest sip out of my own cup and put it aside.

"So, here you are," he says.

"You wanted to see me."

"I did."

"About the primaries?"

"About Bill Scanlan."

"How do you know about Scanlan?"

He winks his eye. "Don't I know everything what goes on in my ward, Jim?" Now comes the butter. When he calls me Jimbo he's being snide. When he calls me Jim it's time for calling in favors. Since Delvin's been my chinaman and got me my first real job in the sewers and in the party, no matter I do a million favors for him he's always got me as an asset on his books. "What do you know about Bill Scanlan?" he says.

"He lives in a flat in a converted loft building over on Morgan, just off West Washington. It sits out there in an empty lot. There's a zipper factory on the first floor and Scanlan's apartment's on the top floor. Also on the top floor is the landlord and a young woman by the name of Joyce Lombardi . . ."

"A friend of that queer dame, Canarias."

I don't protest because Delvin's as narrow as a bird's beak when it comes to sex. People who got different tastes are queers, faggots, lesbos, dykes, fairies, or switch-hitters and not to be invited to sit down in decent company. Which ain't to say Delvin don't have to sit down with Janet at party functions, since she beat him for the alderman's seat in the Twenty-seventh, but he lets her know he don't like it. Also they've never traded favors. Even so, whenever I got to sit still and hear somebody bad-mouth somebody over something like who they want to love, I get a stomachache from holding it in.

"Joyce Lombardi was found in Scanlan's bed, naked and dead," I says.

"But he was out of town."

"He was back in time to do the job," I says. "That's why he's in the slam."

"*Suspected* of murder, which is quite another thing than being indicted for it. What real evidence do they have? A tired man coming home after a long and weary journey only to find a poor naked young woman in his bed? A frightened man who runs off for an hour or two so he can try and sort out the terrible catastrophe which has befallen him? A good Catholic who doesn't try to hide or dispose of the body which even a fool would know is going to get him into a lot of trouble, but runs away and then comes back to face the music."

"Comes back to lie about the time of his arrival," I says.

Delvin waves that away like it's nothing but a minor point. He takes the last swallow from his cup. "Not drinking your tea, is it, Jim?"

While he's starting on my toddy I ask him how come

he's putting hisself out for this Scanlan. I'm hoping he's not going to say he owes the man the favor because Scanlan gave him a deal on a pocketful of junk jewelry.

"I knew his mother, God keep her," Delvin says, and his eyes grow misty in a different way than how they're always watering.

I don't ask when he knew her, before or after his own wife's death. I just accept there was tenderness between them and that calls for special favors in anybody's book.

"It's not that I want to protect a killer if Scanlan proves to be one," Delvin says. "I'd never ask that of you or of myself, Jim. It's just that I talked to the man and he tells me he didn't do it and knows nothing about it. You know and I know the police ain't about to make a special effort to prove him innocent. They'll only look for evidence to prove him guilty. All I want you to do is keep on nosing around. You're so good at it."

15

I go over to the building on Morgan and West Washington. I want to have another look at Joyce Lombardi's apartment to see if I can get anything more out of it now that I know what happened to her.

I take the stairs so I don't announce I'm on my way in the noisy elevator. When I get to the fifth floor I try to walk as quiet as Willy Dink walks. I don't want Kropotkin jumping out of his apartment at me.

I stay along the wall on his side of the hallway and when I get to his door I sneak my eye over to see if his eye's on the other side. It ain't blocked so I quick-step across the hall and open up the orange door with the key Willy Dink gave me, and don't think I ain't been wondering about *that*. I mean if I mention to anyone that Willy Dink's got a key to her flat he says I got a key to her flat and if I say he gave it to me he says I'm a liar. That's very complicated but I wonder if that's the way Willy Dink's little rodent brain could operate.

Joyce Lombardi's flat feels very different now that I know she's dead. I go into her bedroom. I know it's my imagination but the perfume smells fainter than it did before, as though it starts fading the minute she's killed.

I don't think she was killed in Scanlan's apartment. For one thing, Scanlan's bald and wouldn't have no use for a hair dryer. If she was naked, the natural place for her to have been attacked was right here.

But I can't find any clothes dropped on the floor or

tossed in the clothes hamper. She could've hung them up nice and neat when she went in to take a shower or a bath, but I don't think she would've hung up soiled things. Besides, where were her shoes, which she would've kicked aside? Or the panties she would've changed? Or the bra, if she wore one?

I check in the bathroom just to make sure a hair dryer didn't walk back in.

I go through all the drawers in the bedroom but I don't see anything that tells me anything. After a while I feel like a peeper, poking through her silks and satins. For what?

There's no photo albums filled with pictures of herself when she was a little girl, or in high school, or on a picnic with some friends. No pictures of a mother or father on the dresser. No picture of the boyfriend.

In the kitchen there's a box on a shelf next to a small pile of newspapers. It's half-filled with those composite photos in different hairdos and costumes that models and actresses hand out. The stamp on the back says they'd been shot by Miller, the photographer downstairs.

As I walk out through the living room on my way downstairs, I notice the used glass ain't there anymore. I wonder if Forensics took it away with them and if they'd found anybody's prints except hers on it.

There's nobody in the reception area when I walk through the door of Miller's studio.

Somebody yells, "Yo," from one of the other rooms like he's a marine at roll call.

"Yo," I yells back.

"In here," he says.

I walk into the big room with the light table. This skinny guy with long arms and legs is perched like a one-legged water bird on the stool, one toe hooked around the rung. His hair's falling over his eyes while he's shuffling through the photographs of all these pretty girls. He lifts his head and I get a start. His eyes are such a light color for a minute I think he's blind. They're eyes that could scare you if he wasn't smiling in such a friendly way.

"How can I help you?" he says

"Thinning the turkey herd?" I says.

He gives a little laugh. "What do you know about thinning the turkey herd? You in the trade?"

"Somebody told me that every springtime the pretty girls start pouring into Chicago from Iowa, Kansas, Missouri. All over," I says.

"That's right," he says. "All the pretty girls from all the small towns. All the harvest queens and homecoming princesses. All the prettiest girls on the pep squad. Chicago isn't New York and it's not Los Angeles, but it's the big town closest to home. Small enough to learn the ropes and get a start on the way to fame and fortune."

"How come you call them turkeys?"

"You ought to see them when there's forty of them waiting to be interviewed, strutting around, stretching their necks, turning their heads from side to side checking out the competition. Just like a lot of big, beautiful turkeys. And every year most of them get chopped."

I look down at the mess of photos and spot the little pile with Joyce Lombardi's photo on top. I pick them up and shuffle through them. "Did Joyce Lombardi make the cut?"

"You another cop?"

"I'm a friend of a friend."

"Why should I talk to you?"

"The friend's Captain Pescaro," I says, telling a little white lie.

"She got a couple of opportunities the year she came to Chicago," he says, reaching for the photographs. "Two, three years ago. Some print ads, annual-report covers, a local television commercial. She had her ups and downs but she was hanging in."

"Were you picking her out for something?" I says, giving up the pictures.

He glances down at them. "I was thinking about using her and the rest of these girls for a catalog. It doesn't pay anything like top money but the job lasts awhile. Now. . ." He shakes his head like that's all the eulogy he can bear to speak.

"You knew her pretty good?"

He seesaws his hand in the air in front of his face.

"She lived right here in the building."

"This is where I work, not where I live."

"You took her picture."

"I did her composite, yes. I do thirty, maybe forty, a year."

"You do them for nothing?"

The friendly look fades away quick and the pale eyes look very dangerous.

"No, I charge."

"I mean did you do hers for nothing?"

"What makes you ask?"

"I'm just wondering how neighborly you are."

"I charged."

"Than you'd have a canceled invoice in your records."

"Maybe not."

"Well, see, that's what I mean. Maybe you traded favors."

"You say you're not a cop? Then go to hell. Joyce's dead. I don't want to talk about it."

"No, I'm not a cop, but I told you I can get a cop."

He's got a good stare but I'm used to stares and they don't faze me very much.

Finally he gets off the stool and walks past me. "I want a drink," he says.

I follow him into the studio, where he goes over to a steel supply cabinet and takes out a bottle and a couple of plastic glasses.

"None for me," I says.

"More for me," he says.

"You still ain't told me how Joyce paid you for the pictures."

"I charged her but I didn't bill her. You know what I mean?"

"Avoiding taxes?"

"Why not? Most of my business is industrial, commercial, and catalog. I do portfolio shots for models if they ask me. I do them for cash, but I do them for a price."

"You ever take it out in trade?" I says.

"That's blunt enough," he says, sitting down in one of them canvas butterfly chairs and waving me to another. "You think that's how it works, don't you? Guy takes pictures of pretty girls he's got more pussy than he knows what to do with."

"If you're talking about cats we can talk about cats," I says. "If we're talking about women, yes, I think that's the way it works. I hear all the lies about how painters and photographers and gynecologists see so much tit and ass they couldn't care less. So how come there's so many married gynecologists? How come painters got kids? How come photographers walk around with smiles on their faces like cats what got to the cream?"

"All right, so now and then."

"Is it now and then with you?"

"I take what I can get if it's offered."

"That how come you sleep away from home so much?"

"Who told you that?"

I shrug.

"I sleep away from home only when I'm working late," he says.

"You live over to Evanston, don't you?"

"That's right."

"What's your address?"

"What for?"

"Never mind. I can look it up down to City Hall."

"Why do you want to know where I live?"

"I like Evanston. It's a nice neighborhood. Maybe I'll take a walk around, look for a house for my wife and me. Ask a few questions from people here and there about what kind of community Evanston is. Around where you live."

"Talk to my wife?"

"Maybe. Why not?"

He makes this rushing noise with his mouth and knocks back his drink. Then he pours another.

"If you told her you were going to burn me for running around with women, she'd light the match."

"How come you're still together?"

"How come we're still together? We love each other."

He's smiling at me like it gives him pleasure confusing people, but he's not confusing me.

"I understand that," I says.

"Do you?"

"Sure. Mr. and Mrs. Policarpus used to live downstairs in the flat underneath the one I live in, fought all day practically every day. Threatened suicide and murder, depending on the season. When he died, she grieved so hard she was buried alongside him a month later. I gave up trying to figure how people love each other years ago."

"Well then, that's how it is between my wife and me."

"How was it between Joyce and you?"

"Once or twice. It didn't ring any bells. How can you figure? Maybe I just got lost in the crowd."

"She had a lot of menfriends?"

"Plenty."

"That's not what Mrs. Warren says."

"What does that old whore know?"

"She says Joyce was a loner."

He shrugs and makes a face as though the whiskey's going sour.

"She have any special man?" I says.

"A few, I guess."

He pours his third. He's already feeling it, getting surly and mean.

"Was Scanlan one of them?"

"That I couldn't swear to. I mean he's living right in the building. On the same floor. She runs over to his place, he runs over to her place, how am I going to know? You want to know, you should ask Mrs. Warren."

"You ever take Mrs. Warren's picture?"

"Sure," he says, and grins and looks at me with them pale eyes of his like he's not trying to hide a thing.

"That all you want to tell me?" I says.

"That's all I know."

"It wasn't much," I says, getting up out of the canvas sling.

He gets up too. "Sorry. Next time there's a murder maybe I can do better."

"What's that setup over there?" I says, pointing to the table and the backdrop, the camera on the tripod and the mirror and the thing that looks like the barrel of a gun.

He goes over and puts his hand on the barrel. "Laser light," he says.

"What's it for?"

"Making holograms. It's the future of photography."

I say that's nice and go up to talk to Mrs. Warren.

16

I guess she was expecting visitors. Cops and reporters and maybe me. Anyway, she's dressed for the situation in a white satin nightgown she couldn't really sleep in because she'd slip off the bed, an open matching robe over that, and white satin feathered mules on her feet. Her toes, painted red, are peeking through.

She's plucked and penciled her eyebrows which isn't done much anymore, and she's painted her mouth so that it accentuates the little bow under her nose.

"Come on in, Red," she says.

"You know, it's funny," I says. "Nobody's hardly ever called me Red. Not even when I was a kid."

"See that? There's something special between us already. So, you call me Maggie and we're halfway there."

I don't ask her where.

"Sit down and enjoy the view while I make us some refreshment. I'm having a champagne cocktail."

"Would a cup of cocoa be too much trouble?" I says.

"Afraid I'll get you drunk and take advantage of you, Red?"

"It's the middle of the day," I says.

"So it is, so it is," she says and goes into the kitchen, stepping on the pressure plates in the floor that make the light go on.

I go take a chair facing the big window. The sun's in that part of the sky so she's got this gigantic mini-blind angled so it filters the light. Even so I got to half-turn my head to keep the glare out of my eyes.

When she comes back she's got two big champagne glasses in her hands. "I don't want to spill chocolate all over me. Don't worry, yours is plain ginger ale."

She sits down on the couch across from me, crosses her legs, ducks her head, and takes a sip from her glass. I taste mine. It's ginger ale.

"Are you celebrating something, Mrs. Warren?" I says.

"Maggie," she says. "No, it's not a celebration. More like a wake."

"For Joyce Lombardi?"

"Somebody's got to raise a glass to her."

"She ever talk to you about having any family?"

"She mentioned foster homes and guardians who tried to get their paws into her bloomers."

"Where'd she come from?"

"Somewhere around the Rockies." She shrugs as though things like that don't matter. "If there's nobody to see she's buried decent I want to take care of it."

"Janet Canarias is going to see to that," I says.

"Joyce's lover?" Her mouth twists a little when she says it.

"You got strong feelings about that sort of thing?"

"Strong feelings?" she says.

"Are you down on lesbians?"

She busts out laughing. "You got to watch yourself there," she says. "You almost made a dirty joke. No, I'm not down on them. I've had women in my time. Part of the act."

"You have Joyce Lombardi?"

"No, not Joyce. Pretty as she was, those weren't the sort of feelings I had about her."

"What feelings did you have?"

"You ready for a laugh?"

"Whatever you say."

"I felt like a mother . . . like an older sister towards her. No, like a mother. I'm old enough."

"That's not what you told me before."

"Who the hell you think you are, coming around asking questions expecting people to spill their guts to you?"

It looks like my day for nasty drunks. The sun slips down an inch and dazzles me. I blink.

"Why don't you close them blinds all the way?" she says, very sweetly, the perfect hostess. "Just twist that plastic rod at the side."

I go over and work the little gadget what closes them all the way. The light in the room is gray like it's raining outside. When I start back to my chair, she has her head twisted around looking at me. The gloom turns her white skin, white hair, and white satin gown blue.

"How did she feel toward you?" I says.

"I was the faded lady on the third floor. She was polite and friendly, but we didn't get girlish together. I told you that. She didn't confide in me. Not much, anyway."

"Not much, but something?"

"The kind of thing one woman might tell another she'd practically just met. The funny side of life. People share that without much trouble. It's the pain and troubles that's hard for some people to give away."

"She tell any funny stories about Scanlan or Miller?"

"Scanlan took her out a few times. Nothing came of it."

"She did him favors."

"You mean spending an evening now and then with one of Scanlan's business associates?"

"Like that."

"She wasn't selling it."

"You're sure of that?"

"If she was in the trade or thinking about going into the trade she'd have come to me for advice. I never tried to hide it from her, how I made my pile. I couldn't hide it from you either, could I?"

"How about the photographer?"

"She might have slept with him. Why not? He's attractive. Those eyes can get to you."

"They're very weird."

She grins. "That's what I mean. Kinky. Besides, she could've thought he'd give her career a little boost."

"Favor for favor?"

"He does a lot of catalogs. So, a friendly tumble for a leg up. It happens every day. When women take over the world it'll still happen. Only it'll work the other way."

"She ever mention anybody else?"

She opens her mouth like she's about to say something, then quickly lifts her glass to her lips and drains it.

"You can tell me or don't tell me," I says. "When the cops come, you skip a beat like that and they'll come down with the hammer on you."

"They'll have to go through hell getting me to tell them anything I don't want to tell them."

"I'm not out to hurt anybody for the fun of it," I says.

"What are you out to do?"

"Do a favor for a friend and put her heart to rest."

"How's that?"

"Because it's what I like to do."

"All right," she says, making up her mind. "Up until about seven, eight months ago Joyce had a very deep relationship with a man."

"She was in love?"

"That's what she was. You notice how phony saying that sounds nowadays? Books and movies and television have knocked the life out of the words. Nobody knows what they mean anymore."

"I think people know what they mean when they say it themselves."

"You could be right. How the hell would I know? So, Joyce and this man have it bad for each other, but they can't bring it out in the open."

"He was married?"

"Married and in no position to change it. Not for a while. Not till he saw how a certain ball would bounce."

"She got tired of the game?"

"She would've hung in there until whenever, if that's all it would've taken. But if he got his hand on this certain ball there's no telling how long he'd have to run with it. Probably forever."

"So she decided to break it off while the breaking was good."

"It couldn't be good. But it was smart."

"She came to you with it?"

"The first time she ever shared something serious with me. The only time. She had a way about her, you see. Like a kid who needs help building her tree house but who's going to build it on her own all the same."

"So you told her to break it off?"

"I didn't tell her anything. People come to you for advice, they don't want you to tell them what to do. They want you to find out what they've already decided to do and then agree with them. You should know that."

"Sometimes I forget," I says. "So you nodded your head when she told you she was going to end it?"

"And patted her hand and told her she could come down to my apartment anytime she wanted a champagne cocktail or a good cry."

"This breakup happened how long ago?"

"Six months. That's when she said good-bye the first time."

"What do you mean?"

"Good-bye is the hardest word in the world to hear and the hardest one to say. You hear about clean cuts every day but they're very rare. Usually a love affair is cut up with a dull knife, a little piece at a time. He was holding on, Joyce's lover. I suppose he didn't really believe it was over until she told him she was moving in with someone else."

"Did she tell him the someone else was a woman?"

"I don't know. I doubt she'd do that."

"Because she'd be ashamed?"

"Because she'd think it was none of his damned business."

"Something like that could put a man in a rage," I says.

"Because most men are fools," she says.

"Anything else you want to tell me?" I says, standing up.

"Like what?"

"Like the name of this man."

"His name is Charles Frazier."

Charles Frazier is the other party's candidate for governor.

17

After I leave Maggie Warren's I go up to Joyce Lombardi's and let myself in with the key I never gave back to Willy Dink and which he never asked for. I remember seeing some pictures of Frazier in the Sunday supplement of the *Tribune* last week or the week before. I go to the pile of newspapers on the shelf in the kitchen and find the section. One of the photos has been cut out. From the captions I can tell it was one of Frazier, probably a portrait shot. There's a couple of other, smaller pictures of him with other people. I take the page with me over to Kropotkin's.

"You need some more help?" he says.

I show him the pictures and pointed to Frazier. "This the guy who came looking for Joyce so many times the other day?"

I got my finger on Frazier's bow tie, right under his smiling face. Kropotkin reaches over and pushes my finger across about two inches.

"This guy," he says. "I never seen the other one."

I read the caption. It says, "Republican Candidate for Governor Charles Frazier and Aides."

"Is that all I can do for you?" Kropotkin says.

"One other thing. How's Miller's business doing?"

"He pays the rent on time."

"How come he ain't got a receptionist?"

"They come and go."

"How's that?"

"He has receptionists but they don't last too long. You want to ask why, go over to the Rullin mansion. You know, to the museum I told you about. The last one who quit or got fired is working there."

"Who told you?"

"She did. I see her over to Stosh's Saloon one night."

"She got a name?"

"Sure, but I don't remember it."

It takes me half an hour to find a parking place anywheres near close to the Ohio Illinois Insurance building on North Michigan Avenue where Frazier has his offices. I know that he used to run the company but three years ago he steps down as CEO and starts doing good works, pointing his nose toward the governor's mansion. He still sits on the board and they let him use a suite of offices.

Maybe I should tell you a little bit about how the Republicans and Democrats make a deal about the city of Chicago and the state of Illinois. They both put candidates in the field for most of the jobs in the city and state, but the truth is the Democrats expect to win Chicago and Cook County and the Republicans get to run the state.

So, how it works out is, the Democratic party will lend a helping hand to a Republican candidate running for state and expect favor for favor for the Democrats running in the city of Chicago and the county of Cook.

Frazier's suite is on the top floor. I get by the guard at the private elevator by telling him I'm a messenger from Ray Carrigan, the Democratic party chairman. He calls up and the okay comes down in about five minutes.

The doors at the top open onto an acre of marble floor. There's a very cool-looking older woman, dressed in a beige suit, shoes, and stockings to match, who comes out from behind her desk with a smile on her face.

"Mr. Flannery," she says, "if you'll please follow me."

She's got nice long legs and a good stride. She walks half a step in front of me, showing the way, with her upper body half-turned to me like she's the one who's deferring to me. It's one of the moves a person's got to learn in the corridors of power. I'd stumble over my own feet if I tried to do it.

I think she's going to take me all the way, but she hands me over to another, younger woman in a blue suit, with shoes and stockings to match, who leads me along to these big doors which open just as we get to them.

"Mr. Frazier?" I says to the man holding the door. He nods to a man in his late fifties who's sitting on the couch.

Frazier gets up and I can see he's wearing two-hundred-dollar slacks, a hundred-dollar shirt open at the neck, and a five-hundred-dollar sweater.

There's no desk in the room, which is supposed to give everybody the idea that nobody's cutting any deals here. There's a plain tall wooden stool where a desk would be.

Wilkie, the fella in the newspaper photograph, comes over to stand behind the couch. He's watching my hands.

"Mr. Flannery?" Frazier says.

"Have you got any identification on you?" the other fella says.

"I got my driver's license," I says, going for my wallet.

"Never mind that, Mr. Flannery," Frazier says. "We called Carrigan's office but he wasn't there."

"He's probably over to Dan Blatna's Sold Out saloon in the Thirty-second having kielbasa and cabbage," I says.

"That's Big Ed Lubelski's ward, isn't it?" Frazier says.

"That's right. Carrigan goes over there on Wednesdays."

"Nobody in his office knew about any messenger Carrigan sent to us," Wilkie says.

"But they knew a Mr. James Flannery, of course," Frazier says. "Not that you need any introduction, Jim. May I call you Jim?"

"Call me Jimmy if you want to, Charlie."

"Well, Charles, if you don't mind."

Nobody's stuck out a hand to shake yet.

"What can I call you?" I says to Wilkie.

He don't bother answering. Frazier goes over and sits on the stool. "A little trouble with my back," he says. "I can't sit for long on anything low and soft." He still don't ask me to sit on anything low or soft.

"You got in here under false pretenses, Jim." Frazier's face is very tight all of a sudden, his smile gone as quick as Willy Dink chasing a rat. "Do you want to tell me why?"

"I'd like to know when was the last time you saw Joyce Lombardi."

One eyebrow goes up. It's like an actor doing what they call a reaction shot.

"You can waste a lot of time and say you don't know any Joyce Lombardi . . ." I says.

"Joyce Lombardi? Harvey?" Frazier says to Wilkie.

Wilkie's staring at me.

"If you're here to protect Charles, Harvey, why don't you give him some good advice?" I says.

"You can ask *me* when I saw Joyce last," Wilkie says.

"You're a good man, I can see that," I says. "Good at your job . . ."

"I saw Joyce Lombardi the last time about a week ago," Wilkie says, raising his voice a little.

"That's no good," I says. "Joyce told her story to the woman downstairs."

"Hearsay?" Frazier says.

"In a murder case, hearsay don't get convictions but it gets plenty of investigation," I says.

Frazier's face goes white. He starts to stand up off the stool, but can't seem to keep his balance and sits down hard again, almost slipping off the stool onto the floor. Wilkie's over to catch him by the arm and help him over to the couch.

"I went looking for her several times yesterday," Wilkie says.

"You're not listening to me, Harvey," I says. "Joyce Lombardi's been murdered."

"I'm telling you it was me who had the relationship with Joyce."

I stand up and shrug my shoulders. "Okay. You decide how you want to play it. I'll just go talk a little hearsay to the cops. It won't be hard for them to ask the same questions of the same persons I did."

"I could make a few phone calls and have you warned off," Wilkie says.

"You could make a few phone calls but all you'd get would be some promises your contacts couldn't keep," I says. "You ask around. Nobody calls me off I don't want to get called off."

Wilkie moves up in front of me. He's got me four inches and fifty pounds.

"Maybe I could talk to you in a language you'd understand."

"Don't be a jerk," I says. "Take a peek at your boss. He's working out the odds. Any second now he's going to decide . . ."

Frazier says, "Sit down, Jimmy . . ."

"Bingo," I says.

" . . . and let's talk."

18

I expect to hear a story so old I could've told it to him. But his tale's got a twist.

Powerhouse businessman. Two kids grown up and gone away. Success in a business that's starting to bore him. No challenges. Here's the twist. A wife who loves him, but who's a paraplegic because of a car accident. Unable to satisfy a man with normal appetites.

I remember that his wife never shows up at any affairs with him. Her picture's never in the paper. You figure she's a very private person or they've got an arrangement to lead separate lives. If what he says is true, in a way maybe they have.

"I met Joyce at a fund-raiser for Marty Allardick," Frazier said.

"Ran for county attorney. You backed him big."

"He didn't make it. But I considered it money well spent. It showed the party I was prepared to pay my dues. Joyce was in a little tableau dressed up as Uncle Sam. She even had to wear a little tuft of white beard on her chin." A smile flickers across his mouth. It quivers like he's trying not to laugh, or not to cry. I could see the pain the news of her death is causing him. At least that's what I'm supposed to see if he's working me. "There were other pretty girls in the show, but the reason I noticed Joyce was because she winked at me as if she were saying that she knew how silly it all was but there was the rent to be paid."

"So, you offered to pay it?"

"It was nothing like that," Frazier says, glaring at me. "Nothing at all like that."

"You telling me you didn't pick up the tab on that apartment over on Morgan? You didn't pay for the furniture?"

"Of course I did. What could it have come to? Forty thousand dollars' worth of rugs and furniture? Sixteen hundred a month for rent?"

"The way you keep your books, that ain't buying it?" I says.

"When a man has as much money as I have, priorities change. Joyce never asked me for anything. Not a dime. She understood when I told her we couldn't be seen in public. I just wanted a place to go. A place to take off my shoes and kick back." His voice got soft like he was remembering the good times. "I offered to have meals from the best restaurants in town sent over, but she wanted to cook for me herself." If he's working me, he's very good. His eyes're misting up and he almost manages a tear.

"She never asked you to use your influence to help her in her career?" I says.

"Never. She never asked the smallest favor."

"And she never complained that she was the woman in the closet?"

"She wasn't in the closet."

"Next you'll tell me your wife knew about her."

He hesitates for half a beat and then he says, "She did."

I don't know if my mouth's hanging open.

"I was considering a public career. A candidate can do just about anything he wants after he gets into the club, as long as he doesn't do it out in public and scare the horses. But before he wins office he has to be like the pope, above suspicion, above reproach. It can't be known that he has a mistress. It can't be known that his wife consents to it because she loves him."

"There'd be plenty of dirty jokes," I says.

"Nobody would understand, or want to understand, that such an arrangement was settled upon for the best of reasons, to save a marriage."

"Was Joyce happy with the setup?"

"I didn't intend for it to turn out the way it did. We fell in love. I said we'd work it out after the election, win or lose."

"Joyce would become the wife, and your ex the friend?"

He tapped his forehead with a finger. "All things are possible in the landscape of one's dreams."

"But Joyce knew if you made governor all of that'd never happen, so she broke it off."

"She broke it off, but I thought I could talk her around."

"But she didn't talk around. She found somebody new. She walked out of the apartment you set her up in. Walked out with nothing but the things she walked in with. The television. This and that. Put them in storage maybe. I should've figured a girl like that wouldn't have a pink nude on her bedroom wall. That was you."

"No, it wasn't me. Do I look the sort? What does it matter anyway? She didn't tell me she was going to live with another man. She said Wilkie's persistence on my behalf made it essential for her to find some room, so she was going to stay with a girlfriend."

"Janet Canarias was more than a friend," I says.

He frowns and looked at Wilkie.

"There was no other man," I says, putting the point on it.

He don't have to hear it three times to get my meaning.

"You been having Wilkie call her a lot?" I says.

"Several times a day for several weeks. Then he stopped because she wasn't picking up. I called myself, many times, but all I got was her answering machine."

"She wasn't answering her own phone. But she had to answer when she moved over to her girlfriend's place because any calls coming in could be for the friend. So, you got the referral number, whether she wanted you to have it or not, and you called the new number. Joyce picked up and you finally had a chance to talk her into meeting you."

He sits there saying nothing, just shaking his head.

"You found out that she was giving you up to enter into a love affair with a woman. I don't think you could handle that. I think you met with her the other night, had a fight, and lost your head."

"If Mr. Frazier had made contact with Joyce, what was I doing going over there knocking on her door?" Wilkie says.

I give him my innocent look. "Hey, I don't know everything," I says. I stand up.

"Where are you going, Jimmy?" Frazier says.

"Well, I got my regular job to do."

"But we haven't reached an agreement yet."

"What agreement?"

"How we're going to handle this problem."

"What problem's that?"

"My friendship with Joyce Lombardi."

"The way we handle it is, if you murdered her, me or the cops or somebody is going to find a way to hang it on you. So you'll go to trial and maybe you'll get convicted."

He nods his head like he's pleased to be having this conversation with a reasonable man. "I'd expect nothing less," he says. "I'm asking you if my name can be kept out of this until you, the cops, or somebody decides that I should be charged with Joyce's murder."

"Still worrying about your run for the governor's chair?"

"Still concerned about protecting my wife, Mr. Flannery. You can believe that or not, as you please."

19

When I get back to Polk Street there's a little Model A Ford truck with a hand-built camper on the bed parked in front of the stoop. It says "Willy Dink's Natural Vermin Control" on the side panel. There's a coat of arms with a mailed fist, a snake, a ferret, and a terrier in it, and a ribbon with some words in Latin which I don't understand.

Stanley Recore, the kid who lives across the hall from Mary and me, is sitting on the stoop with some other kid I don't know. Then I see it's Willy Dink hisself.

Stanley spots me and comes running over all excited like he gets and telling me in this way he's got of talking—which ain't exactly an impediment but which is a way of saying words that, unless you knew, you'd need an interpreter—all about his new friend.

"Jimbly, Jimbly," he says, "Willy Dink has been tellin' me abou' a snick that eats meece and a dog what whestles wats." Which means that Willy Dink has a snake that eats mice and a dog that wrestles rats.

"How are you, Willy Dink?" I says, holding out my hand to shake.

"Not good," he says, putting a limp paw into my hand.

"What's the matter?" I says. "Where's Timmy?"

"Well, that just it, ain't it? They took Timmy and Max and Herschel away and put them in the slam."

"Max?"

"Max is the king snake and Herschel is the ferret. Also

they got Shirley, Paulette, and Millicent under lock and key too. Every creature I got is gone and I'm out of business."

"Who done it, the Board of Health? Animal Control?"

"The cops done it. A pair of cops by the name of O'Shea and Rourke. Well, O'Shea done it. Rourke didn't seem to like the idea very much but there wasn't much he could do."

"Tell me what happened."

"Well, I was getting down to the fine work over to Kropotkin's when this O'Shea puts the arm on me. Grabs me by the back of the neck like I was a rodent and gives me a shake. It was humiliating and also somewhat painful."

"What was his gripe?"

"That's what I asked him. 'What's your gripe?' I says. 'What are you doing sneaking around the scene of the crime?' he says. 'I don't know nothing about no crime,' I says. 'I'm just filling a contract.' 'Hold on,' he says, 'you mean to tell me you don't know there's a woman been murdered in this building?' 'Oh, I know that,' I says, 'but I don't know nothing *about* it.' 'What would you say if I told you I don't believe you?' he says. 'I'd say that was your problem,' I says. 'I don't want to be the only one with a problem,' he says. 'Show me your business license. Show me your exotic-animal license. Show me your health certificate, you're going into places where they cook and serve food. Show me . . .' "

"I understand," I says, afraid that Willy Dink's going to go down the whole list of every license and permit on the city list, which he ain't got any of. "Come on upstairs and I'll make a couple of calls."

I go up the stairs with Willy Dink following me and Stanley following Willy Dink. It's like a parade.

Mary's home. She says hello to Stanley, who asks her if she's got any chawpee. She says he's too young to be drinking so much coffee and how about a glass of milk.

Stanley takes what he can get, especially after she tells him there's peanut-butter cookies to go with it.

After I introduce him, Willy Dink says he'll have the same.

When I go to the phone, Mary says, "Ray Carrigan's office called you and wants you to call them back."

"In a minute," I says.

I dial the police station and get through to Pescaro right away, like he's waiting for me.

After the usual I says, "How come O'Shea took Willy Dink's animals away from him?"

"They're against the law."

"A dog's not against the law."

"A dog without a license is against the law."

"Mr. Dink's been giving me a list of the permits and licenses you say he's supposed to have to stay in business."

"See how easy it is?" Pescaro says.

"It'd take him a month of Sundays to get all them papers."

"Then he better get started because, if I got it right, the animal people only hold impounded animals for a week, ten days, and then they dispose of them."

"We're talking about a man's livelihood here."

"I'll tell you what, Flannery, you keep your nose out of police business and I'll see what I can do for your friend."

"Oh, oh," I says, "what am I hearing? Somebody put the fix in?"

"I don't know what you're talking about," he says.

"For God's sake, Pescaro, the man's a Republican."

"So, think it over. Either get something for minding your own business or get charged with obstructing the police in their investigation."

I hang up and stand there thinking about how Pescaro could be thinking. He knows threatening me only makes me hold on like a junkyard dog. So maybe he *wants* me to keep looking in places where *he's* been told *not* to look. One thing I know about Pescaro, he wants to be a good cop, but he understands if you try to go head to head with the politicians you'll get chewed up and spit out without a gold watch or a pension. So he's taught himself a lot about skinning cats.

Next I call up my chinaman, Delvin. The phone's picked up after about twelve rings and it's Mrs. Banjo.

"Mr. Delvin is not at home," she says.

"This is Jimmy Flannery, Mrs. Banjo," I says. "Where is he?"

"Oh, it's you," she says. "Hold on, I'll see if he just stepped back inside the door."

I hear a voice and after a long minute Delvin clears his voice in my ear. It sounds like Mrs. Banjo had to wake him up. "How's your lovely wife, Jim?" Delvin says.

"I'm sorry if I disturbed your nap," I says.

"Think nothing of it, Jim. I catch forty winks now and then so my mind'll be fresh when I'm awakened in the middle of the night ready to serve my constituents."

"It's four o'clock in the afternoon," I says.

"I wasn't speaking in the particular but in the general," he says. "Servant of the people, ever awake. And how can I serve you?"

"I have a friend . . ." I says.

He interrupts me to say, "This is not a friend who needs a place to keep pigeons?"

"No," I says, "this is a friend what keeps snakes and ferrets."

I tell him about Willy Dink's problem and when I'm through Delvin says, "What's this got to do with sewers?"

"I thought you could steer me to the right man."

"This is a matter for Dunleavy."

"What has Streets and Sanitation got to do with snakes and ferrets?"

"When all is said and done, my boy, nothing's got anything to do with anything except skeletons and juice."

"Skeletons," I says.

"Knowing where they're buried. Go see Dunleavy in person. A visit's always better than a telephone call."

There's a pregnant pause.

"By the way," Delvin says.

"Yes, sir."

"You can forget about looking into that matter concerning my friend Bill Scanlan."

"You're letting him drown?"

"I'm letting justice take its course," he says in this righteous way he has sometimes, and hangs up in my ear.

I get through to Carrigan quicker than I got through to Pescaro.

"Jimmy," Carrigan says, "are you playing cops and robbers again?"

"I'm doing a favor for a friend."

"More like cops and killers, right?" he says, like he didn't even hear me.

"Alderman Canarias asked me to look into the death of a friend."

He still don't hear me. "If you want to be a cop, Flannery, why don't you take the test? Even at your age, I think we could maybe use a little influence and put you in blue."

"I'm happy doing what I'm doing, Mr. Carrigan," I says.

"That's smart. It's smart for a man to be contented with his place in life. Then all he's got to worry about is keeping it."

So, Frazier ain't trusting me to keep his name out of it. He makes a few calls and asks a few favors. What the poor sucker don't understand is that he just jumped into their pocket.

Or maybe he understands and is willing to pay the price.

"So, when do I get my babies back?" Willy Dink asks me.

"It's going to take a little longer than I thought," I says. "You finished?"

He wipes a mustache of milk off his mouth and brushes some crumbs off his sweater onto the linoleum. He thanks Mary and trots out after me.

Stanley stays behind to have another cookie and make goo-goo eyes at Mary, who he's got this terrific crush on, young as he is.

When we're standing downstairs next to his truck, I don't know what to say. Willy Dink's standing there like a lost soul with nothing to do.

"Hey," I says, "I like your camper."

"I sleep in it," he says.

"For God's sake, don't let O'Shea catch you."

He shakes his head and looks forlorn.

I tell him to meet meet me around the corner right after supper that night so I can tell him how I made out with Animal Control.

"Hey," I says, "what does that motto on your coat of arms mean?"

"It's a sort of free translation," he says.

"Yeah?" I says.

"It says, 'Let us get the buggers before they get you.' "

20

Mary makes a meat loaf with double-baked mashed potatoes. It's a special occasion. My father, her mother, Charlotte, and Aunt Sada are coming to dinner.

Mike and the two ladies go everywhere together. It's only May and already they're making plans to take in as many of the neighborhood summer events they can squeeze in. Events like the carnival over to Twenty-sixth and Kostner, the Fiestas Patronales in Humboldt Park, and the Dorsey Gospel Festival down on South Shore Drive.

The three of them are together so much Mary and me call them the Musketeers. They giggle like three kids when we call them that. Well, Aunt Sada and Mike giggle. Charlotte's more sedate.

One time Mike and Aunt Sada come over wearing mouse ears. Mary explains that we don't mean Disney we mean Dumas and my old man says he never met the man.

The special occasion which calls for meat loaf is what Mary likes to call a family conference. I don't tell her I hate the idea of family conferences because that only means they're all going to sit around and decide that I'm not doing something I should be doing or whatever I'm doing I shouldn't be doing or I'm doing wrong. Also they're always having family conferences on these television sitcoms where everybody sits around making the old man look like a damn fool, and I hate them things. If we was sitting around making Mike, who's *my* old man, look like a damn fool maybe that wouldn't be so bad, but I'm the man of my own house so it's me what gets the needle.

I could call a halt to it if I wanted, but I can't really call a halt to this occasion because Janet Canarias has become like best friends with Mary, and Mary fights like a tiger for those she considers her own. She's baking meat loaf because she wants a family conference about Janet Canarias.

Just to be sure I got it right, I says, "Is Janet coming over?"

"No."

"Well, how come she ain't—"

"Isn't."

"—invited?"

"I thought somebody might start talking about her friend and that would only spoil the evening for her."

"I don't think so. I think she wants to talk about Joyce Lombardi every chance she gets. I think she wants to feel the . . ."

"Who wants to feel pain like that over and over again?" Mary snaps.

"I wasn't going to say 'pain.' I was going to say 'rage.' She talks about Joyce and thinks about the murder and builds up a head of steam."

"She wants justice."

"She wants blood, and she don't care whose it is."

"That's not true."

"Oh, yes, it's true. She don't know it's true, but it's true. Until somebody dies for her friend's death she won't get any sleep. And, when something like that's driving you crazy, it gets so you want to sleep more than you want justice."

Mary looks at me like she's trying to figure out what I'm trying to say.

"I've got to be very careful," I says, "who I point the finger at."

About an hour later, when we're all sitting down around

the table in the kitchen, I says practically the same thing. I also says, "She's been very good at the job since she took office. The people like her and even the old politicians—except for one or two old diehards—like her. Even though they can't figure out how come. They'd like to do her a favor if they can do her a favor. But they don't want to step on any important toes."

"I need a translator," Aunt Sada says, leaning across the table at me, her auburn hair whipping around as she shakes her head.

Mike's grinning at her. "So, you don't know everything about politics even if your late husband—"

"Late *lamented* husband," Sada says.

"—was the secretary of the Socialist party."

"For six years before his death," she says, practically jumping in his face. "Politics I know. This what we're talking about is favoritism. The arrogant, cynical trading of privilege and immunity." She whips backs to me. "If I'm hearing you right, what you're saying is Canarias is pushing for an arrest, trial, conviction, and maybe an execution."

"She's pushing hard and she's pushing everybody."

"Somebody else, somebody who knew this Joyce Lombardi, is paying, one way or another, to be left out of it. One minute you were told—"

"Asked."

"—not to look too hard at this Scanlan fellow who lives next door to the dead woman found naked in his bed. The next minute somebody says never mind saving Scanlan. Back to Canarias. She's pushing so hard she could push her way right through to this important man who I notice you don't mention his name."

"I gave my word to keep his name out of it unless I got evidence against him."

"All right, you gave your word and I won't ask. So, what we've got is a question. Is it possible the powers that be would just as soon hang it on Scanlan or any other poor noodnick who'd make a likely candidate just so they can satisfy Canarias and this important person at the same time?"

"It sounds Byzantine," Charlotte says.

"It's Chicago. It's big-city politics and it happens every day," Aunt Sada says. "It happened in the beginning and it'll be happening at the end."

She leans back and smiles all around, especially at Mike, letting us know that when it comes to the twists and turns of Chicago politics, she may be getting old but she ain't slowing down.

She leans forward again and cocks her head. "So, okay, now let's get down to the nitty. Let's have the details. Leaving names out if you made promises."

"I only made a promise to the one person."

"So tell us the players on your scorecard."

I start out with Kropotkin and mention the ax, the way he likes to peep, the deal he's got with Mrs. Warren—which sounds to me like she's paying with her favors for the extra protection he gives her—the fact he's got keys to every apartment and closet in the building and that he spoke about Joyce Lombardi in the past tense when I first talked to him.

"That sounds like a very lonely man," Charlotte says.

"And men who live alone get a little funny in the head," Aunt Sada says, tossing a sideways look at Mike.

Then I tell them about Mrs. Warren, who I figure was a whore and then a madam. Who saved her pennies for her old age and ended up, without friends or family, in a luxury flat furnished in white. Who slops around in an old flannel robe and slippers when she's by herself and dresses up like Jean Harlow when she's hoping for company. Who tells me one time that she don't know Joyce Lombardi too good and then tells me she felt like a mother to her.

"Women who live alone get very strange," Mike says.

Aunt Sada holds up another finger. "Anybody in the

building's got opportunity. But, I'm having trouble seeing a motive for this widow, madam, or whatever she is."

"I think maybe more people kill without a reason than with one nowadays," Mary says.

"Ain't that the truth," Mike says.

"I think there's always a reason underneath," I says. "Maybe it's just somebody's mad at the world and they take it out on the first person they come across."

"The next player," Aunt Sada says.

I tell them about Miller, the photographer. How he took Joyce Lombardi's pictures for her composite.

Charlotte asks and I tell her what a composite is.

I tell them how he's having trouble at home over to Evanston and stays at the studio on Morgan more than every now and then. I tell them about what he said about thinning the turkey herd, which is a cynical thing to say but also could be sinister if you looked at it a certain way. I say how he told me he had all the beautiful women he needs or wants, that he slept with Joyce a couple of times but nothing clicked.

"Did you believe him?" Mark says.

"It could happen. I mean he's in a profession where pretty girls are all over the place, all of them hungry to get somewhere and plenty willing to do whatever they got to do to get there."

I tell them about his funny eyes.

"Funny eyes is good," Mike says. "You can tell a lot about a man from his eyes."

"How about a woman's eyes?" Aunt Sada says, staring at him.

"Also a woman's."

"What kind of reasoning is this that you can tell a man's a killer from his eyes?"

"You saying you can't look at some of the pictures of murderers they print in the newspapers and see it in their eyes?" Mike says.

"When you already know they're murderers you can

see it. If you didn't know you'd probably say they were bank tellers or grocery clerks. I won't accept the eyes. It's a feeling but not a clue. Have you got any *clues* about this photographer?"

"He's got a busy business and a receptionist's desk, but he's got no secretary."

"How do you know that?"

"I nosed around the desk. There wasn't any of the things in it that women keep in desks."

Mike makes a sound like steam escaping.

"So, that's a clue," Aunt Sada says, and holds up another finger, telling me to go on to the next suspect.

I tell them all about Willy Dink and his animals and how he creeps around without making a sound, listening to the rats in the walls.

Charlotte gives a little shiver. "Let me help you clear the dishes, Mary," she says.

"I've got to hear this, Mother," Mary says.

"Willy's got keys to everywhere," I says. "I think he could slip through a crack even if he didn't have a key."

"That's my man," Mike says. "That's the killer."

Aunt Sada ignores him. "What do you think, Jim?"

"I could make a case against him. He had opportunity. Maybe he even had a reason."

"What reason?" Mary says.

"Say this little man with his dog and his snake and that other creature slips into Joyce's apartment after she comes back from Janet's for whatever reason. Maybe he's already there when she comes in and decides to change her clothes."

"Why would she do that?" Mary says.

"She was going to start a new life with Janet," I says. "When Janet comes home Joyce's going to be there waiting for her. With the lights low and the music playing maybe. With drinks and dinner ready maybe."

"A romantic setting," Aunt Sada says.

"Maybe she thought about how she was going to look

for this big moment all day. She packs her bag. One minute she thinks she'll meet Janet in what's she's got on. Play it casual. The next she thinks she'll dress for it. So she goes home to change and Willy Dink comes into the bathroom when she's there naked."

"And then he killed her because she was something he could only dream of having," Mary says in a soft, sad voice.

"Was there evidence of rape?" Charlotte says.

"There was no sign of semen or . . ."

"We're not eggs. We don't break if you say a word."

"No sign of penetration," I says. "But there was some bruising."

"Willy Dink," Mike says. "He couldn't perform and got frustrated."

Aunt Sada tosses him another look as if to say how typical of a man to kill a woman because he couldn't make love to her. "Did she struggle?"

"It didn't look that way."

"And this Willy Dink is a very little man?"

"If she was being choked with the hair-dryer cord from behind, maybe he could have done it."

"Such a little man," Aunt Sada says, holding up the fourth finger.

I start telling them about Scanlan. How he lives right down the hall from this beautiful young woman. How he was a good-looking fella once and still considers hisself a ladies' man, that's pretty clear. He took her out more than once but claims he never slept with her, they was just friends. Good enough friends that he worried about how she could pay the rent, as if he didn't have an inkling that there was somebody paying the rent on an apartment like that. Good enough for him to do what he calls favors for her by fixing up dates with business associates and other friends of his.

"You know what that sounds like," Mike says.

"I know what it sounds like but I'm not ready to draw

the line between what makes somebody a blind date and a call girl. If I was to make a bet I'd put my money on Joyce just getting fed up every now and then hanging around waiting for this important man to find time for her, so she goes out for dinner and maybe a little dancing."

"And maybe takes a little rent money, a little grocery money."

"There you go again," I says.

"There I go where?" Mike says, wide-eyed.

"There you go making a remark, and pretty soon you'll turn it around and make out like it was me called her a dirty name and you who's defending the poor girl's honor."

He looks at Aunt Sada and Charlotte as though astonished at this attack a son's making on his own father.

"That's what you do, Michael," Charlotte says.

"That's right," Aunt Sada chimes in. "Hooker, no hooker, what does it matter? If she was selling herself would that make it right for somebody to strangle her?"

Before we get into an argument about that, I tell them how Scanlan comes home pretending that he's walking through the door for the first time, but how he made these mistakes that prove he's a liar.

"What mistakes?"

"He dumped his dirty laundry from his suitcase into the clothes hamper. He made hisself a whiskey and water and drank most of it."

"And that's it? That's all the suspects we got?" Aunt Sada says.

"Except for anybody who could have been working late down in the zipper factory," I says. "Except for salesmen and deliverymen and the guy what reads the gas meter. Except for any of the grifters, gonifs, and gimps that're thick as fleas in the neighborhood."

"Except for a city filled with dopers, kids, and madmen who'd kill you for a dime," Mary says. "One of them could walk in off the street and kill a person because a car going by splashed his shoe."

21

It used to be I could work out of my head. Do this, do that. Have everything, or nearly everything, done by the end of the day. Now I got to make lists because Mary says that's the way for a busy person to organize his time.

I usually got three lists.

Things to do for the flat like shopping for groceries if I got the time and Mary ain't. Fix the washer in the faucet in the kitchen sink. Take the cleaning to the cleaners. Do the laundry over to the Laundromat. Take a look at a washer and dryer so I can make recommendations to Mary when she goes with me to make the purchase. At which time she'll buy what suits her anyhow, because what do I know about washers and dryers?

It used to be I ate out a lot and dumped my laundry at the cleaners the same time I took a pair of pants or a sweater to be cleaned.

The second list is things I got to do around the job. The job in the Sewer Department, not my job as a Democratic party precinct captain in the neighborhoods. The regular job list is usually very short, because most of it is routine and I ain't getting so forgetful that I miss inspection schedules or forget to follow up on complaints.

The other job, which is the third list, can get pretty long because there's a lot of people who can't, won't, or don't know how to get the system to work for them.

Every time a new mayor sets up another department or agency to take care of a social need or ailment, the first thing they do is have forms printed which not even lawyers can make head or tails out of. Then they hire a big bunch of otherwise unemployables to translate the instructions for people what are hurting so bad for food, heat, or shelter that they'll be ready for the hospital or the morgue before the help they need gets put in the pipeline.

At times like the present I also got a fourth list, which is supposed to be like the notes real detectives take down to help them tie their shoes.

So, lately, with all these lists to organize my time, I never finish even a small part of all the things I got to do every day. I even waste half an hour moving the things I didn't get to do today over to the list I won't get to do tomorrow.

I really understand this kind of time-management stuff because I know how Kippy Kerner's been supervising Ollie Tchinooski when he adjusts the valves on the furnaces in the County Building for the last twenty years. Kippy carries around a clipboard and checks off the list each time a valve is turned on or off just like the copilot checks the pilot when they go through the preflight routine.

It's a wonder how some people can make a job for themselves, although Kippy Kerner ain't the best I ever seen. The palm goes to Billy Swinarski, who sits at a desk in front of the city treasurer's office, and anyone who needs to ask where's the city treasurer's office Billy tells them.

Anyway, I put my lists together first thing in the morning and they tell me I'm supposed to get my good dark suit out of the cleaners and buy myself a white shirt with a button-down collar and a black tie for the funeral this afternoon over to Graceland Cemetery, check with Dunleavy about Willy Dink's problems, which I also figure will give me a chance to ask about who and why there's this shield around Charlie Frazier and like that.

I've got a short list of things that're bothering me.

Like, how did Frazier come and go around their little love nest without being seen?

Like, how come Miller had no receptionist?

Like, where were Joyce Lombardi's clothes?

Like, did Mrs. Frazier know that Charlie was playing around and did she even care?

Like, what happened to the glass in Joyce Lombardi's apartment?

Like, were the cops ready to see a connection between these other three would-be models and Joyce Lombardi's death, and even if they could, how would that help me find out who killed her?

22

Some people say that when they opened City Hall in 1853 they had to get Wally Dunleavy's grandfather's permission. Also the promise that the offices of Streets and Sanitation would be the building's heart forever and ever.

In order to get to the heart you got to go through a maze of corridors that zigzag like a drunken alderman, doors that seem to open up into closets with nothing in them but other doors and staircases that don't go to the floor where you expect them to go.

When I make it to the perimeter, I give the high-sign and the big hello to twenty people I've known since I was a kid, a very few of which will look me straight in the eye. They pretend not to even see me. That's so old man Dunleavy can have fun with his trick which he still thinks, after all these years, fools and astonishes everyone.

Which is, his people alert him to the person who's on the way and Dunleavy gives the order that he wants the latest gossip on the party to be telephoned in to him right away.

So by the time I knock on his door with the grimy pebbled-glass window in it he's primed.

"Come in," he says.

He's sitting at his desk, which is piled high with maps and plats. He leans back with his red-ink ball-point in his hand. It's plain that I've interrupted him while he was moving city blocks, railroad yards, saloons, and churches around like a kid with a Monopoly game.

"It's Jimmy Flannery, is it?" he says. "Mike's kid?"

"Yes, sir," I say.

"Spitting image," he says. "That red hair."

"Mike's hair has been white for twenty years," I says.

"How time flies. So, the jungle drums inform me you're ass-deep in corpses again."

"Only one. A young woman."

He crosses himself and says, "May the Lord keep and preserve her, the poor thing." He gives me a look with his best eye. "I understand you might be offending a very important politician with your shenanigans."

"I'm not trying any shenanigans. I'm just trying to find out who killed her."

"And are you saying the police don't want to find out?"

"I wouldn't say that, but I would say they think they already got the guy what does it and ain't looking any farther."

"So you think you know better than the cops? If they was to come down into the sewers and tell you how to do your job, would you thank them for it?"

I give him a grin and says, "I'd let them do it for me."

"Well, that comparison didn't travel too good," he says. "What they're afraid of is this, Jimmy. Amateurs go poking around, stirring things up, offending important people, and there's always an extra mess to clean up after the case is closed. You can understand that."

"I do. But, what I don't understand quite so easy is how come my chinaman asks me to help him do a favor for this William Scanlan, who's sitting in the slammer, and then has a change of heart."

"Maybe he came to his senses. No sense betting on a horse on its way to the knacker's yard."

"Does that mean Delvin knows that Scanlan did it?"

"It just means he can't be sure he didn't."

"And it's not because he wants the case closed shut, no matter what, so he can do a favor for Charlie Frazier?"

"Frazier's a Republican," Dunleavy says, trying to put me off.

"About to run for state office. That practically makes him a Democratic asset."

"There's that, of course."

"But what I want to know is if Frazier's promised to do Delvin and Carrigan some special favor."

Dunleavy puts down his pen and says, "Sit down, Jimmy. Sit down. Move them books of maps down to the floor and have a seat right there."

I do like he says.

He leans forward and looks into my face. I notice a very sad expression in his eyes. "Don't let it happen, Jimmy."

"Let what happen, Mr. Dunleavy?"

"Don't go getting cynical and bitter. Every politician ain't crooked and every cop ain't in somebody's pocket. There's ways of doing things and ways of not doing things."

"You want to get along you got to go along?" I says.

"That's the way it works, son. But that don't mean the mayor or the commissioner or the party chairman or your friend Captain Pescaro would cover up the murder of your friend Canarias' ladylove just to do a favor for a Republican. You got to poke around, you do it easy. Don't go around knocking over any apple carts and don't go around hurting any feelings."

So Dunleavy's warning me off too.

"Thank you very much for your good advice, Mr. Dunleavy," I says, standing up. "I'll remember what you said. On the other hand, my dear mother—God rest her soul—used to say, 'Every cripple does his dance,' and I guess I'll just end up doing what I got to do." I bend down to put the books of maps back on the chair where he can get to them. He picks up his pen. Life's about to go on in this office where time stands still. The only way anybody'll know I was there is that some dust'll be cleaned off the chair.

"By the way," I says, before walking out the door, "a friend of mine has this little problem."

"This a friend what keeps snakes, weasels, and other exotic pets?" Dunleavy says.

"Well, they ain't exactly pets. They're more like his livelihood."

"Catching rats?"

"That's what he does and from all I know he's very good at it."

"From all *I* know his methods are old-fashioned and he ought to get hisself a face mask, some traps, maybe some of that poisoned bait or even a spray gun and a tank of poison gas."

"I talked to Willy Dink about his profession and he says you bait an infested house the rats die in the walls and make a hell of a stink that lasts a long time. Same thing with traps. Some of these big rascals, come in from the sewers and the lakefront, could drag one of them traps around their neck before they choke to death and then you could—"

"Have them in the walls again."

"That's right."

"You ever think of becoming a lawyer, Flannery? You got the silver tongue."

"I don't put much trust in lawyers."

"Well, there you are, you could be the first honest lawyer to practice in Chicago. What do you want me to do about this friend of yours?"

"I thought you might put in a word."

"I'm not about to trade a favor for a rat catcher. What I'll do is, I'll point your nose the same place I pointed it when you was trying to help that voodoo lady what had a bathroom full of pigeons and pigeon poop."

"I should see Mrs. Wilomette Washington?"

"That's the person." He looked at me with his head cocked to one side like a street sparrow. "Were you expecting me to do you the favor and go talk to the woman myself?"

"Well, I never met Mrs. Washington and . . ."

"And I did. Well, it's because I did that I ain't going to meet her again. She tried to bury me in paperwork once and I ain't going to give her the chance to do it again."

"You could at least find out for me if the Health Department signed the complaint after O'Shea picked up Dink's animals."

"That I can tell you. It did."

He turns away from me back to his maps and plats. He don't look at me but I know he's grinning like a fool, pleasured by the thought that I'd soon be meeting the lady who almost done him in with the same avalanche of forms his department makes a person fill out every time you want to move a tree.

On my way over to the Board of Health I see daffodils on the flower peddlers' carts. I buy two bunches, a buck apiece. One for Mary and one for Mrs. Wilomette Washington.

When I get announced by a secretary and I'm into her office, I hand the flowers to her with a smile which I hope will charm her.

She looks at me from behind the kind of eyeglasses they used to wear what are pinched on the nose. Which is something I ain't seen since I was a kid in the first or second grade and Mrs. Oberlin used to wear the same kind of glasses on a silver chain pinned to her blouse with a little silver clip. Every time a kid—a lot of the times me—cut up or didn't pay attention, she'd do this thing with her eyebrows and make the glasses drop off her nose. At first this made you want to laugh, but then when you got a gander at the icy stare of her naked blue eyes you gave it another think.

Mrs. Washington's eyes are soft brown, but still I'm wondering if she can do the same trick.

"Is this a bribe, Mr. Flannery?" she says.

"Is it working?"

"In what way 'working'?"

"Are you ready to smile favorably on my request?"

"When I hear the request, I'll give you an idea."

She sits back in her big worn leather chair, a handsome woman of sixty or thereabouts with the kind of intelligence shining out of her face that tells you she should be running something bigger than a city health department.

I tell her all about Willy Dink, Timmy, Max, Herschel, Shirley, Paulette, and Millicent.

"You did that very well, Mr. Flannery," she says.

"Did what?" I says as innocent as a lamb.

"You told that story as though it were a fairy tale, anthropomorphizing all those creatures by giving them names."

"Ah," I says, not exactly sure what the word means but pretty sure what she's getting at. What she's getting at is that I'm not pulling any wool over her eyes.

She goes on. "Who but a villain would condemn Herschel . . . By the way, what is a Herschel?"

"A ferret."

"And a Shirley?"

"I think she's an armadillo."

"So, who but a witch or an ogre would condemn Herschel, Shirley, and Paulette to incarceration?"

That one I know. "It's not just they're caged up. According to the rules they could be destroyed."

"Animals require licensing. Exotic animals require permits. That's my understanding."

"Willy Dink's one of them people out there living on the edge. How much money can a man, living with a terrier, a snake, and some other creatures in a homemade camper on the back of a pickup, make hunting rats? He starts paying for licenses and permits, this and that, the competition drives him out of business. So, please, don't give me thirty forms to fill out . . ."

She smiles. "Mr. Dunleavy," she says.

"You remember the situation?"

"Oh, yes. Mr. Dunleavy came in here thinking he'd

charm me out of my shoes with a passing wave of his fine Irish hand. Just like you're trying to do. May I say, you do it so much better? No, I won't load you down with forms to be filled out. You're in the wrong church and the wrong pew. You wasted a quart of olive oil. Your beef's with Animal Control. That's in Maywood."

"I could use whatever help," I says.

She looks down at the yellow daffodils she's holding in her lap by the plastic wrapper around the stems. She lifts them to her nose and takes a sniff.

"It's really spring, isn't it, Mr. Flannery?" she says.

I nod toward the daffodils. "That's what they say."

She lays the flowers on her desk and takes out a piece of paper with her letterhead on it. She writes out a couple of paragraphs and hands it to me.

It's a request to the animal-control officer asking for the release of Mr. Willy Dink's animals to the custody of Mr. James Flannery who she is sure will see to it that Mr. Willy Dink arranges for the necessary permits and licenses. She says how much she and the Health Department will appreciate it, which is like saying she'll owe a favor.

"I'm sorry. Maybe I didn't make it clear," I says. "Willy Dink ain't got the kind of money . . ."

She does the trick. She raises her eyebrows and her eyeglasses pop off the bridge of her nose.

"Mr. Flannery," she says. "There's charity and there's the law. Asking cooperation is a small favor and I'll be glad to assume it. Waiving revenue is a large favor and you'll have to work that one out with Mr. Lukakis for yourself."

23

It's a long drive over to Maywood where they got the city pound. The minute I step out of the car I can smell animals. For a minute there I think it wouldn't be a bad idea if I tied a daffodil under my nose because I know the smell's going to be worse inside the building.

There's a kid about eighteen sitting behind the counter wearing a pair of coveralls with the Animal Control patch on the pocket and the sleeve.

"How many do you want?" he says.

"How many what?"

"How many dogs? How many cats?"

"I want one little fox terrier, one king snake, one armadillo . . ."

He holds up his hand and shuffles through some papers on the counter. "You Willy Dink?"

"I'm here representing Mr. Dink."

"You his lawyer?"

I don't say yes, I don't say no. Sometimes I notice people think you're a lawyer they let you have what you want.

"Can you box Mr. Dink's animals up, or however you do it, and I'll be on my way?" I says.

"Hold on. What do you mean box them up? You expect me to hand them over?"

"If you'd be so kind," I says, the way I think a lawyer would say it.

"You got an authorization?"

"Of what nature?"

"Of the nature of a court order."

"I've got something that serves the same purpose."

I hand over the letter from Mrs. Washington. He takes it out of the envelope, reads it, and shakes his head. "I don't know what I can do about this."

"It's pretty plain, ain't it?"

He lifts his head at that, and right there I know why Mary's forever correcting my grammar. I think that maybe I'll start taking a class in night school, clean up my English.

"I'd like to see Mr. Lukakis," I says.

"Oscar?"

"If that's his first name, it'll have to do."

"I don't know if he'll see you."

"We'll know when you go and ask."

"He's over by the exhaust chamber."

"The what?"

"The place where they put the dogs and cats to sleep."

"I thought you killed them by injection."

"Well, we do. Sometimes."

"When the animal lovers squawk?"

"Injections are very expensive. We go back to using the chamber when the budget gets tight. They just pass out and go to sleep," he says, trying to convince himself it's an easy way to go.

"Don't you say 'kill' or 'die' around here?"

The kid looks troubled.

"I'd rather say 'put to sleep,' " he says. "It really doesn't hurt them, do you think?"

I let it go. I snatch the letter out of his hand and tuck it back into its envelope. "Just point me the way."

"I'll call him and see if he can talk to you now," the kid says, reaching for the phone.

"What's your name?" I says, very hard. Sometimes this makes people stop doing whatever they're doing you don't want them to do. It gives them reason to doubt themselves and start wondering if maybe you're somebody who can cause them trouble and that's why you're asking for their name.

"Henry."

"Henry what?"

"Henry Hackinaw."

"So, Henry, how about I walk through that door and down the corridor. Will that get me to Oscar?"

"Sure, but I think I should tell him . . ."

I don't bother waiting for what else he's got to say. I'm through the door into the heavy smell of cats and dogs.

On one side, facing the back, there's a line of small cages, one on top of another, for cats, raccoons, rabbits, and other small animals. Then there's a long line of narrow pens for the dogs with trapdoors at the back so they can get out into these short runs. It ain't the Ritz but, then, Animal Control's one of the city services what gets cut every time there's a budget slash. So I guess they just do the best they can. All these dogs come crowding up to the wire, yapping, whining, wagging their tails, and waving their tongues at me, like they know what's in store for them at the other end of the corridor unless me or somebody else gets them the hell out of there. It's enough to break your heart.

There's this one pup, what Mike'd call a Heinz because it's got fifty-seven breeds in it, who's too proud to throw himself all over the fence and the floor trying to catch my eye and maybe a pat. He just sits looking at me, quivering a little, like he's thinking maybe he *should* make a damn fool out of hisself, but just can't bring himself to do it even though his life could depend on it. He'd rather keep his dignity.

I look at the wall because I can't stand looking at all these animals that've been abandoned just like some of the poor people I see sleeping on the grates.

Then I hear Timmy and I stop. He's in this cage just like all the others. He's looking at me and hopping around like a kid who knows his mother's come to take him home from his first day at school. I bend down and stick my fingers through the wire so he can get a smell of somebody he knows, but I don't tell him everything's all right because I don't know if it is.

"Wish me luck," I says, and stand up. He gives me a look as I walk away like what's a friend who broke bread with him doing walking away on him and leaving him behind bars.

The door at the other end of the corridor leads to a breezeway. I go through another door and I'm in the place where they kill the animals.

A man in a rubber apron comes out of another room inside this room, taking off a pair of heavy gloves. He's got a face like a pit bull, mean eyes sunk into folds of flesh, a forehead that's corrugated like an old-fashioned scrubbing board, a bunch of hair growing out of the top of his head like a weed patch. He's also got a bad mouth, which twists and turns when he talks, like he's trying to save up spit.

"Who are you, what do you want, and why're you scaring my help?" he says.

"My name's Jimmy, Oscar. Can I call you Oscar?"

"You can call me anything you like, just don't try to butter me. You'll find out I'm a tough mouthful to chew. Tell me what you want or get out of here. I got work to do."

"I understand the work you do can be very hard on the nerves."

"Maybe it'd be hard on your nerves. It ain't hard on mine."

"So I can't appeal to your good nature?"

"I ain't got a good nature. It's all bad."

"So, I can't appeal to that maybe I can appeal to your pocket."

He plants his feet and folds his arms above his belly. "You're a politician."

"What makes you say that?"

"The first thing a politician tries to do is buy you. So, I'm listening."

"Does that mean you're ready to be bought?"

"It means I'm listening."

"I want to get Willy Dink's creatures out of the slam."

He holds up a beefy hand. He's one of them finger counters like Aunt Sada. "That would be one fox terrier, one king snake, one armadillo, one raccoon, one ferret, and one Chinese chicken."

I hand him the letter from Mrs. Washington. He looks it over and hands it back. "So what? These people sign a complaint one minute, lay these animals on me, then change their minds the next?"

"The director of the Health Department is asking you for a favor."

"I ain't going to give it. We're talking big bucks here. Every one of those beasts had to have shots. Rabies. Distemper. Hepatitis and what-have-you. Then there was special tests for pullorum, rhinotracheitis, ear mites, and arbovirus infections."

He's working me. I know it and he knows I know it.

"Next thing you're going to tell me is you had to check for Rift Valley fever." That stops him in his tracks. "Make me a price," I says.

He goes over to a desk in the corner and pulls open the top drawer, rummages around inside, and comes up with a piece of paper. "I got it right here. Mr. Dink wants his animals and that Chinese chicken, it'll cost him six hundred twelve dollars and eighty-six cents. That includes the exotic-animal permits and licenses for the dog and cat. Also he's got to bring me proof that he's not running a zoo to which he charges admission within the city limits. Also that he's not running a poultry farm."

"That's the best you can do?" I says.

"Make it six hundred even. I won't charge for the ants I had to buy for the armadillo."

"That's still too high," I says.

"So go talk to City Hall. That's the cost of services rendered. And in case you're thinking otherwise, not a penny of it goes into my pocket."

He's standing there waiting for me to offer him a fifty or a hundred so he can kick me out. I know the type, self-righteous, mean, and narrow. Would never take a dime, but won't give an inch.

"Willy Dink ain't got six hundred dollars," I says.

"You got six hundred dollars?" he says.

"Not right this minute."

"Well, if you're going to pay the fees you got seven days. That's how long we keep them before we put them down."

He walks straight toward the door at my back like I'm not even there. I step out of his way and go trotting after him across the breezeway and into the smell and clamor of the kennels. I go by Timmy's cage without a glance because I'm ashamed to be leaving him there.

Lukakis goes right to the cage with the proud pup in it, unlocks the grate, and scoops him up.

"Hey!" I says.

"Hey, what?"

"What do you think you're doing with that dog?"

"His time is up," he says in this flat voice.

For the first time I notice there's a red tag on the cage.

"Wait a minute. You can't do that."

"I got to do it," Lukakis says. "You think I want to do it? You think I like to do it?"

I see there's a soft side to this Oscar and maybe that's why he acts so hard. Maybe otherwise he couldn't do what he's got to do.

"I'd just as soon do the people as the dogs and cats sometimes," he says. "They let their pets go making kittens and puppies because they don't want to pay the price to have them neutered or because they just don't care. They get a dog for the kids and when summer's over and they leave it on the beach and go away. They buy a bunny for Easter and the brats manhandle the poor thing until it gets sick and then they dump it on the first blade of grass they come across."

"Couldn't you give that one a break?"

"What? Another day? What's another day?"

"Maybe somebody'll come and adopt him, you give him another day."

"Nobody'll adopt that mutt. Don't you know nothing about orphans? He's too old, too quiet, and too goddamn independent. People come in here looking to adopt a dog, they want one that slobbers all over them."

"Jesus, what's it all about?" I says, reaching out and laying my hand on the dog's head.

He don't shake it off. He don't wiggle it to get a scratch behind the ears. He just looks at me in this solemn way like Bishop O'Herlihy looked at me the day I took confirmation in St. Pat's over to the Fourteenth when I was thirteen. It was like the bishop knew what a terrible sinner I was, and that I'd do wrong more often than I'd do right. But he loved the sinner, even if he hated the sins, and understood my weakness and forgave me in advance for whatever I was going to do.

"That's nice," Lukakis says in this sarcastic voice.

"What's nice?" I says.

"You're humming him a hymn, he shouldn't die without a little celebration."

"I wasn't humming . . ." I start to say, and then I realize I was. Under my breath I was humming this tune from a movie picture I saw once with this English actor in it. *Alfie* was the name of the picture and the song. "Oh, yeah," I says.

"I got to tell you, Alfie," I says to the dog, and he cocks his head a little like he knows I mean him. "The landlord's going to have a fit he ever catches you peeing in the hall. No pets allowed. That's the rule. Then there's Mary. I don't even know if she likes dogs."

"You saying you're going to take him?" Lukakis says.

"That's right," I says, snatching Alfie from his arms.

"He ain't free, you know."

"I already got that picture," I says.

We got to the front office and while he's giving me the license tag and the papers, and I'm giving him the cash, I says, "How about you give me a break on Willy Dink's creatures?"

"Six hundred bucks," he says, and that's that.

24

Alfie's sitting next to me in the car and looking out the window like he's saying, "Hello, world. Didn't think I'd make it did you?"

Every once in a while he looks at me for a second like he wants to know is it okay for him to celebrate, and I pat his neck to reassure him. He starts a little each time, like this could be the hand of doom, then he relaxes and looks out the window again like he wants me to know he trusts me to do the right thing.

I'm on my way over to Forensics. The business about the missing glass is on my mind and I want to make sure Forensics picked it up when they swept Joyce's apartment.

I get lucky and find a spot at the curb on a street close to the crime lab over on South State. I crack the window so Alfie can have a little fresh air while he's waiting, and I go looking for Harold Boardman.

I find him with his eye stuck into a microscope. When I clear my throat he looks up at me with this dreamy look in his eyes.

"Necrotic tissue," he says.

"Oh?"

"From a body buried on the site of an old tannery. Very interesting."

"I'll bet it is."

"Can I do something for you, Flannery?"

"The other night over to William Scanlan's?"

He nods.

"After you finished tossing his place did you go have a look around the victim's apartment down the hall?"

"That's standard procedure," he says, nodding his head and pushing his glasses up higher on his nose with his middle finger.

"You see the glass on the coffee table?"

"I can't remember any glass on the coffee table. Let me check the book."

He goes over to a bookcase and picks out a loose-leaf binder with "Lombardi" and a case number printed on the canvas cover in black ink. He pages through it, shaking his head as he checks the inventory. "No glass." He looks up at me and his eyes ain't dreamy anymore. "Was there a glass, Flannery?"

"I thought there might have been."

"Were you in the victim's apartment before and after the murder?"

"I had a look around. I was . . ."

He waves his hand. "You don't have to explain yourself, Flannery. I'm not going to blow the whistle on you. But maybe you'll want to tell Pescaro you were in there yourself because he might notice the fact on the record."

"How's that?"

"Would you mind stepping over here to the table? I've got to take your prints."

"What for?"

"We lifted sets all over that apartment. Then we made a file of everyone we knew had been on the scene one time or another. That way we start cutting down the unknowns."

I let him ink and roll my fingers.

"So, how many unknowns you got?" I says.

He shrugs. "Early times, Flannery."

I wipe my fingers on a piece of paper towel and start to go.

"That's two you owe me, Flannery," Boardman says.

"What office are you running for?" I says.

"You never know."

While I'm going out to the car I think about taking his advice and talking to Pescaro. It don't seem like such a bad idea. It makes me look cooperative. Also I'll get to ask a couple of questions of my own.

Alfie's glad to see me. He wags his tail and blinks his eyes when I give him a pat.

On the way over to the station I says, "You know what we got here, Alfie? We got a beautiful girl what has been murdered by somebody who couldn't complete the act of rape."

Alfie gives a little whine and I look at him in surprise. It's the first word he's spoke. While I got my attention on him a cab comes out of a side street making a turn right in front of me and blowing his horn like I'm the one in the wrong.

"It's awful the way some people drive, Alfie," I says.

He don't say anything but keeps his eyes straight ahead like he's saying if I won't watch the road, he'll do it for me.

Pescaro ain't overjoyed to see me.

"The nod the other night was just for the occasion," he says. "It don't mean I handed you a badge."

"The nod was to show Alderman Canarias that the police were being cooperative. So, why change her mind?"

"All right, what do you want?"

"First I want to tell you I was in Joyce Lombardi's apartment."

"When was this?"

"After Chips Delvin asks me to see what I can do for Scanlan."

"What you can do for Scanlan is bake him a cake with a file in it."

"You think you got him cold?"

"What do you think?"

"I think I see a used glass in the Lombardi apartment the first time I'm in it. Before her body's found. I think I *don't* see it this last time I take a look. So, I go down and talk to Boardman over to Forensics and they don't know anything about it."

"So, that's why you're here confessing—"

"I'm not confessing anything."

"—to illegally entering premises under seal?"

"What seal? Her apartment's not a crime scene."

"It is . . . in a manner of speaking," he says.

"Never mind scolding me," I says. "Keep to the point. There was a glass and now there ain't a glass. Somebody took it away because they was afraid it could be used in evidence."

"That kid Boardman don't know everything. He don't know some of his coworkers ain't as conscientious as him. One of them could've picked up the glass to get himself a drink of water. Then he flashes to the fact that he just spoiled some prime evidence. So he dumps it."

"Give me a break," I says.

"It happens every day, Flannery."

"You mean the Chicago Police Department is less than perfect?"

"Now you're being smart and I ain't got time for smart. Use the door."

"I got a couple of questions."

"You're not on this case. You work in the sewers, goddammit. I got a backed-up drain in the street in front of my own house as a matter of fact. Why ain't you out there taking care of it?"

"You find out anything about the three models found dead this year?"

"What've they got to do with Joyce Lombardi?"

"She was a model."

"Now *you* give *me* a break, Flannery. I ain't got enough trouble, you're trying to hang a serial killer around my neck? Go talk to the Central Investigation Unit over on State Street."

"I just came from State."

"So, go back."

"You telling me you got a dead model in your district and you ain't asked for the file on them other three?"

He's very good at hiding, but he ain't that good. His eyes go flat and I know he's going to lie to me.

"You trying to make a package because they was all models? For God's sake, Flannery, we got three plumbers murdered, you're going to say there's a nut out there killing nothing but plumbers?"

"I'd think about it."

"There's no connection, Flannery. Go bother somebody else."

Back in the car I says to Alfie, "Go bother somebody else. Go talk to Central Investigation. How much you want to bet we go see Central Investigation they give us the runaround. Can't find the files or who the hell do I think I am, asking to see them in the first place."

Alfie shifts in the seat so he can lean against the door and look at me.

"What I was talking about before? You know, about what we got with this poor murdered girl? We got Charlie Frazier. Maybe he gets mad because he wants to have another tumble in the hay to convince her she shouldn't give him up and she refuses him. So he tries anyway and can't do it. So now, he's got that to make him even madder and he grabs the first thing he can get his hands on—maybe the dryer's on the nightstand next to the bed—and wraps it around her neck. Or maybe Joyce decides she's not walking out with nothing. She decides to shake him down a little. He sends Wilkie to reason with her."

I take a look and Alfie smiles and lets his tongue hang out a little bit.

"You're not convinced," I says.

He gives a little yip.

"You hungry?" I says.

He stands up and wags his tail.

"Okay, we'll have a little something and then go on over to Frazier's house and nose around a little bit."

I find this hamburger joint which has got a patio with some benches and umbrellas. It's not all that warm, but there's no wind blowing, so we decide to sit outside and have a couple of hamburgers. I get a soda for me and a dish of water for Alfie. It's nice sitting there talking to Alfie. It's like having a partner riding around with me.

"Also we got to go see Scanlan over there in the slammer. Maybe he's scared enough he'll tell us something he ain't told anybody yet. In fact, we'll do it first."

25

When the guard walks me down to his cell, Scanlan comes up to the bars smiling like I was his brother or, at least, a long-lost friend. The guard lets me in, then closes the door and walks over to sit on a stool in the middle of the corridor.

"Jeez, am I glad to see you," Scanlan says.

"How's that?"

"Mr. Delvin told me he'd put his best man on the case and see I was sprung out of here."

"He said that, did he?"

"How soon will it be?"

"Well, I don't know. It's early times," I say just like Boardman says to me.

Scanlan sits down on the bunk, letting his disappointment show, jiggling his legs like he'd like to get out and just keep running until he dropped. I sit down next to him.

"I know how you feel. How far have they gone?"

"What?"

"Have they arraigned you yet? Did you stand up in court and identify yourself as the man named in the complaint? Did they read the charges and advise you of your constitutional rights?"

"This morning," he says.

"They set bail?"

"My lawyer's out trying to make it."

"Who's your lawyer?"

"Manny Inkle."

I nod.

"He's good, isn't he?" he says, looking for any ray of sunshine. "My accountant tells me Inkle's very good."

"Your accountant?"

"He's the closest friend I got."

"Manny Inkle's very good and he won't steal you blind. How did you plead?"

"Jesus Christ," Scanlan says, crossing himself. "I pleaded innocent, what do you think?"

"When's the preliminary hearing set?"

"A week. Well, six days."

We sit there not knowing what else to say.

"You must be a very close friend of Mr. Delvin's," he finally says, like it's just something to break the silence.

"He gave me my start in politics," I says.

"He used to know my mother. After she was widowed. Maybe they slept together. I don't know. You don't like to think that about your mother."

"Well, if mothers never done that, we wouldn't be sitting here talking."

"And I wouldn't be up for murder. Anyway, he was the most important contact I had in the city, so I called him."

"I know, and he asked me to see what I could do for you."

This pitiful grin brightens up his face for a second. "Yeah." Then it goes away like a cloud comes back over the sun. "So, how come he doesn't answer my calls? How come he won't talk to me anymore?"

I don't know if I should tell him somebody with more juice'd got to Delvin and Delvin had washed his hands.

"You know, don't you?" Scanlan says.

I wonder why I'm trying to save Delvin's butt.

"Somebody more important than you asked him to leave good enough alone and not go around pushing the cops to look elsewhere."

"So they're tying the can on me," he says sadly, as though there's nothing much he can do about it now. Almost like an afterthought he says, "You happen to know who this more important person is?"

"Charlie Frazier," I says.

"Son of a bitch. That rotten son of a bitch," he says.

"What's got into you?"

"Frazier's the one who was paying Joyce Lombardi's bills."

"How do you know that?"

"He used to come see her by way of my apartment."

"How's that?"

"He only came at night, after Miller and the people from the zipper factory were gone home. He didn't want to be seen. He had a way into the basement and rode the dumbwaiter up to my place. All he had to do then was walk down the hall and nobody the wiser."

"How come Kropotkin never saw him?"

"I don't think Kropotkin's got his eye to the spyhole twenty-four hours a day. He probably takes a peek only when he hears the elevator or somebody knocking on Joyce's door."

"How come you didn't mention this up to now?"

"I knew it was over with them. Besides, while it was going on, he was paying me a hundred dollars a week for the use of my door. He's still paying me. And, then, there was promises."

"Promises?

"You know, for after he was governor?"

I get up and he looks at me like Alfie looked at me when he was in the cage.

"Anybody come visit you?"

"Miller from downstairs."

"I didn't know you was friendly."

"We're not. He said he just came to be neighborly. Came to cheer me up a little. He didn't cheer me up." He blinks at me like he's going to cry. "I wasn't supposed to be back from this last trip for another week," he says. "If I hadn't cut it short, I wouldn't be in this goddamm mess."

I say good-bye and walk out thinking how whenever something bad happens to a person they ask themselves why they stopped to tie their shoe or didn't stop to answer the phone.

26

Frazier and Wilkie, the vaudeville act, could've been working me pretty good. It's a good story about the crippled loving wife and the sweet and willing mistress. But how do I know it's true? There's nothing much about Mrs. Frazier anywhere. Just a couple of scraps about a boating accident fifteen years ago in the newspaper files on film at the library. She could easy be a bitter bitch who wouldn't stand still for the little threesome he claims she wanted as much for her as for him. It's the kind of prop to a story that, if you knock it out from under, brings the whole con tumbling down.

I drive over to Lake Shore Drive to the condominium where the Fraziers live when they're in the city. You buy a closet in a building like this and it sets you back a hundred thousand. I don't want to think what the whole floor near the top, where they hang their hats, would cost. You brood about things like that and the next thing you know you're unhappy with what you got. You get greedy and pretty soon you're studying to be a lawyer or a Wall Street takeover pirate.

A doorman opens the front door for me. I give him the nod. He gives me a little lip curl which could be a smile or could be he don't know if I'm a tradesman or what.

I go over to the security post in the middle of the ocean of marble where another guy in uniform sits watching a dozen television sets with pictures of entrances and corridors on them. I'm surprised to see it's Danny Maroon. For over twenty years he was the night guard over to my old girlfriend Poppsie Hanneman's duplex on Lakeview.

"How you keeping, Mr. Flannery?" he says.

"No complaints, Mr. Maroon," I says. "What's a nice fella like you doing in a joint like this?"

"Daylighting."

"You still work over to Mrs. Hanneman's?"

"Oh, sure. This is just for a little extra. In a couple of years the wife and me figure we'll have enough."

"Enough for what?"

"Enough to retire down to Florida. We're going to raise Dobermans for guard duty."

"You always liked dogs."

"I mentioned that, did I? You here on business or pleasure?"

"I want to go upstairs and knock on Mrs. Frazier's door."

"Ooops."

"What does that mean, Mr. Maroon?" I says. "Is that Doberman talk?"

"That means I got orders not to allow anybody upstairs without written permission."

"How do the groceries get up there? How does their dry cleaning get delivered?"

"We know all the deliverymen."

"How about flowers?"

"Him, too."

"Maybe the florist hires a temp."

"So, I'd call the florist to check. Then I'd have to call upstairs anyway."

"Give me a minute, Mr. Maroon," I says.

I turn around and go out the door again. "I was checking the address," I says to the doorman. "I got to go to my truck. I'll be right back."

"Take your time," he says, and gives me the full lip because now he makes me for a delivery boy.

I walk down the block to a fancy florist there. It costs me twenty bucks for a bouquet of spring flowers. I'm wondering who I'm going to get to pay for them. Here I'm spending twenty to deceive somebody and all I spent on Mary's daffodils was a buck.

The doorman don't open the door for me this time, I got to do it with my hip. I go up to the desk and slip Maroon a folded twenty.

"Here you are, Mr. Maroon," I says, "a little something to bring the sunshine a little closer. Do me the favor and tell them upstairs there's some flowers coming up."

"Well, I don't know, Mr. Flannery."

"You know me a long time, Mr. Maroon. You know I'm not out to do anybody any harm. And ain't I done everything I could to keep you covered?"

"You've always been a thoughtful man," he says, and snatches the twenty while the doorman's loafing against the wall and staring out the door. He makes the call and after about a minute nods to me and points me toward the elevators. "Take the one on the right, that's the service car, and when you get to the fifteenth go down to the door at the end of the corridor."

I go up in a freight elevator that reminds me of the one over to Joyce Lombardi's building. The same canvas pads on the wall and the same noisy machinery. I get out on the fifteenth and walk over to the front door. I ring the bell and stand there with the flowers in front of my chest. After a minute a voice says, "Go to the service door," through a little speaker in the wall.

"Huh," I says. "What's wrong with this door, lady?"

"I said go down the hall to the door at the back."

"Go back where? You don't want these posies, it's okay by me, lady."

Chicago deliverymen are not known for being outstandingly polite so I know the maid on the other side of the door ain't going to think I'm acting funny.

"Down the back," she says, getting impatient.

"Go back downstairs? You got to talk plainer. This talking through microphones is okay if you can understand mush."

The door flies open and a good-looking woman about twenty-five is standing there in a dark dress with a white collar and cuffs. "Clean out your ears," she says, "I speak plain enough."

"I just wanted to see the pretty face that went with the pretty voice," I says, giving her a smile.

"You could've seen it just as good at the back door to the kitchen. That's where deliveries are made."

"Is that what you are trying to tell me? You ought to have somebody look at your speaker," I says, staring at her mouth so she'll get my meaning.

She reaches for the flowers. "All right, you've had your look. Now hand them over and go on about your business."

I pull the flowers out of her reach. "I was told to deliver these personal."

The laughter in her eyes starts to fade. They get filled with suspicion instead. Her left hand settles on the wall beside the door out of my sight.

"You better dump those flowers on me and back off or you're going to be up to your ears in blue serge," she says.

She's ready to push the alarm button alongside the door. I got no idea what that'll bring down on me, but it won't be good. I back off a step, to give her room, so she won't feel threatened. I'm trying to think of something to say to calm her and distract her when a voice comes from inside.

"Who is it, Mary?"

"My wife's name is Mary," I says, trying to let her know I was just flirting around, having a little fun.

"It's a man with some flowers, Mrs. Frazier," she says, turning her head so she can look down the hall inside.

I use the second to take a step alongside her and move around so Mrs. Frazier can see the flowers.

"Well, take them from him," Mrs. Frazier says.

"He claims he was told to deliver them personally."

"Oh? Has he got red hair?"

"Yes, ma'am."

"She's about to push the alarm, Mrs. Frazier," I says.

I hear the whine of a motor. Mary steps away. Mrs. Frazier, sitting in one of them electric wheelchairs, stops inside the door and looks at me with a half-smile on her face.

"Flannery?"

"Yes, ma'am. Jim Flannery."

She reaches for the flowers and I let her have them. She smells them and smiles all the way. "I wonder if it wouldn't be a good idea for the police to bring flowers when they come to question someone."

"It'd surely improve their image, which most people think is pretty crude," I says.

"Come in, Mr. Flannery. Come in and let me tell you the truth."

"Do you want me to put those flowers in water?" Mary says.

"I think I'll keep them in my lap for a little while," Mrs. Frazier says.

She turns the chair around and I follow her down the polished wood floor to a room filled with sun and expensive furniture. There's a big full-length portrait of her when she was young and on her feet above the fireplace mantel. She parks herself right under it, daring me to make the comparison.

When she was young she was so beautiful it would've stopped your heart. The years and the pain and sitting in a chair ain't taken any of it away. They've just shaved the ivory finer and finer until it's like a light shines through her skin.

"You were expecting me," I says.

"Charlie told me you'd probably be coming around. He's a good judge of what people will do."

"I don't know. He tried to warn me off."

"And you didn't warn off. Give him a break, Jimmy. He'd only looked you over for five minutes before he asked you to give up trying to pin Joyce's death on him. Sit down. Do you want anything? A drink? Coffee?"

I shake my head. "I just want the truth you mentioned," I says, sitting down in a chair that costs more than our whole living room.

"The truth is just what Charlie told you. I not only agreed to Charlie taking a mistress, I was the one who first mentioned it and urged it on him. Are you shocked?"

"I don't get shocked. The only people what get shocked are the ones who expect other people to live up to their ideas about what's right. I just look at what's what without making up my mind about what it's supposed to be ahead of time. If it hurts somebody else, it's bad. If it don't hurt anybody, it's even. If it does some good . . ." I let it drift off.

"Do you disapprove, then?"

"It happens every day."

"No. What happens every day is that husbands take mistresses without their wives' knowledge. At least most of them believe the wives won't find out. They do, of course, sooner or later. First they know and then they find out."

"So, what you're asking is do I disapprove of you going along with it?"

"Of being one of the architects of the arrangement," she corrects me.

"Mrs. Frazier, I'm not smart enough or wise enough to

say one way or the other. I think a doctor would say one thing and a priest another thing and a hooker on the stroll something else altogether."

I glance at her and she smiles. "I know the language," she says.

"We've all got appetites and hungers and feelings that got to be satisfied," I go on. "We also got all kinds of laws and no-nos, that ain't actually on the books, meant to keep us from smashing into each other. I don't know what happened between your husband and Joyce Lombardi."

She starts to say something, but I don't give her the chance. "You don't really know that either," I says.

She keeps quiet.

"The two of you thought you was renting a body to satisfy some of Charlie's needs," I says. "From your point of view it was a loving thing to do. I can't argue with that. From Charlie's point of view it was satisfying a physical necessity. I can't argue with that either. But then you got to look at Joyce Lombardi's point of view. I'm not saying she didn't think it was a great deal—it was a lot better than some things young women got to do to get by—but you weren't hurting a part of a person, you were making a deal with a whole human being. And that, maybe, wasn't such a loving thing to do."

"Do you want to hear the details?" she says.

"No. Not unless telling them to me'll comfort you in some way."

"No. It won't."

"Then I don't have to stick my nose in your private business anymore. I'm satisfied." I stand up.

"Satisfied that Charlie had nothing to do with Joyce's death?"

"Satisfied that you knew about the arrangement. Hey, what works for Charlie works for me. I only had five minutes to size him up, so what can I tell you?"

"Thank you for the flowers, Jimmy."

"You're welcome," I says. "See you around?"

"That well may be," she says. "If Charlie goes ahead with his candidacy, I don't intend to hide in the background anymore. We might be sitting shoulder to shoulder at some political fund-raiser."

"I'm a Democrat."

"So what?"

I smile and says, "You're learning the game already."

27

"Also we got the fact that Scanlan could've killed Joyce because he tries to make it with her and she won't have him even though, like he maybe says to her, she's quick enough to do it with these dates he fixes her up with," I says.

Alfie looks at me very interested. It's amazing how he picks up what I'm saying right where I left off.

"I'm not forgetting Willy Dink," I says. "You want to go looking for a frustrated man, you couldn't do better than Willy Dink."

Alfie makes a little noise in his throat.

"Oh, I know. We always got Kropotkin. Also Miller with them funny eyes. And then, what else you got, is you've always got the passing stranger."

We think that one over. I drive up in front of my building and park the car.

"Well, we're home, Alfie. Now, Mary's here, but she could be taking a nap before we go to the funeral. I ain't going to tell you how to play it. I'd never ask you to make yourself a fool. But a little smile maybe wouldn't hurt."

I pick up the daffodils, which are a little the worse for traveling around without water, and get out of the car. I go around the other side and open the door for Alfie and he hops out.

"You got to do a little something before we go inside?" I says.

He goes over to the telephone pole and lifts his leg.

"Well, okay. We got that done all right."

I look around to see if Stanley's around. Because, if Stanley's around, he'll make such a fuss word'll get back to the landlord sure as hell. I go up the stairs to my door with Alfie trotting at my heels.

"I got an idea," I says. "Can you hold these?"

I put the stems of the daffodils into his mouth. He holds them very easy and don't squash down on them.

"So, sit right here," I says, and point to the spot right in front of the door. Then I ring the bell and duck off to the side.

When Mary opens the door she's wearing her robe. "What in heaven's name?" she says.

Then I show myself.

"Who's this?" Mary says with a big grin all over her face.

"This's Alfie. He brought you a present."

"Who does he belong to?"

"That's up to you."

She stoops down and takes the daffodils out of Alfie's mouth, not even mentioning anything about the landlord. Alfie's tail starts to wag and he smiles and moves a little closer to her. She puts her arms around his neck and he looks up at me like he's asking me what am I doing there spying on a tender moment.

We go inside.

"We can make him a bed by the hot-water heater," Mary says. "You better get ready for the funeral. I've already had my bath."

By the time I'm showered and dressed, Mary's in her dark suit and hat.

There's a knock on the door.

When I open it up, Stanley's standing there.

"I hear you got a dog, Jimbly," he says. "You wan' I should take it for a walk?"

28

Doing what I do, I attend too many funerals.

Janet's keeping this one very simple. No viewing the body in the casket. No chapel ceremony. Just a gathering at the graveside over to Graceland and a few words before they put Joyce Lombardi in the ground.

There's maybe a dozen and a half people there besides Janet, Mary, and me. Kropotkin, Mrs. Warren, Mr. and Mrs. Frazier, Wilkie, Miller, and a hard-eyed bleached blond standing next to him who I figure could be his wife. There's a little man who looks very Jewish and five women who are plainly Latino. It looks like maybe Joyce had made the acquaintances of the people in the zipper factory, or maybe they was just showing their respects for a dead neighbor they hardly even knew. The way it was in the old days.

Also there's a very smartly dressed older woman and three young ones who are beautiful enough to be models and probably are.

While the minister's saying Godspeed and something nice about the dead woman, Kropotkin sidles over and stands next to me.

"You see that pretty old hen with the pretty young chickens?" he mumbles.

"Turkeys," I says, without thinking.

"What?"

"Never mind. So, what about her?"

"She's the one who came looking for Joyce the day after she disappeared."

"Who's the one standing next to Miller?"

"That's his wife."

"Did she know Joyce Lombardi?"

"I don't know. Could be. She came around the studio every now and then. That's how come we got introduced."

"And the little man with the Latino women?"

"Mr. Manules, owns the zipper factory, and some of his machine operators."

So, I was right about everybody, but what did that get me?

After everybody who wants to throws a handful of dirt on top of the coffin, the little groups around the graveside start breaking up. Mr. Manules herds his workers down the slope to a van and the woman with the herd of beauties starts toward a rented limousine.

I go down on a line that'll cross theirs.

"Excuse me," I says.

The older woman turns to me and sets her feet like she's posing. The younger women take positions six feet away in a semicircle, their feet turned out a little too, one leg in front of the other like a bunch of big beautiful birds. It all comes so natural.

"Was you a friend of Joyce Lombardi's?" I says.

"I was her agent," she says.

"Was you over to her apartment looking for her the day before she was found?"

"I went there two days before the announcement was made in the papers and on television."

"Thank you," I says.

She touches my sleeve.

"Are you a policeman?"

"No, but I'm trying to help them find who done it."

She looks at the pretty bunch of women standing there, lifting their heads. Their hair, all different colors, blows around their smooth cheeks and softly painted mouths when the breeze springs up off the grassy hillside.

"I pray that you do," she says very soft. "There's a terrible amount of danger that goes along with the gift of beauty."

She turns away and the proud, lovely creatures step their way carefully down to the big black rented car with the rented liveried chauffeur waiting with his hand on the latch of the door.

I go back up the hill to Kropotkin.

"Do me a favor," I says, "go say something to Miller."

I'm a step or two behind him when he reaches the photographer and starts talking to him. I move so I can shake Mrs. Miller's hand and move her off a little ways.

"I didn't know Joyce too good," I says. "Are you a relative?"

"I'm Connie Miller. My husband owns the photography studio in the same building that Joyce lived in," she says, looking at me with one plucked eyebrow raised high.

I'm not saying that every person's history and nature is written on their faces. But there's some who give you a pretty good idea of who and what they are by even a quick look at their eyes and nose and mouth. Connie Miller looks like the kind of woman men would say was hell in bed. She's also the kind that could cut your throat and never blink. She's got the kind of mouth you want to fall into, even though you know she can bite nails in half, and the kind of eyes that's always half-laughing at you.

"Then you was a friend of Joyce's?" I says.

"I met her once or twice. I think Jerry took some pictures of her."

"But you weren't friends?"

She starts walking down the slope with me alongside her, leaving her husband and Kropotkin behind.

"Do I look like a mouse?" she says.

"How's that?"

"You don't look like a cat. So, stop playing the game."

"I'm willing if you are."

"I've got no game to play."

"You've got a husband who maybe strays."

She laughs and covers her mouth like she don't want to let it out and maybe fall down and roll around the ground.

"If he could learn something from it, I'd probably tell him to be my guest. Just so long as he brought it home afterward. If you're trying to make the case that Jerry had anything to do with Joyce's death, that he killed her during a lovers' quarrel or something, you're barking up the wrong tree. Jerry has troubles that way."

"What way?"

"With his equipment. He can't always make it work. Especially I don't think he could make it work with anybody except me."

I'm thinking that a thing like that could give a man an even better reason to go into a rage if a woman was to laugh at him, but I don't say it.

"Still asking questions, Flannery?" Miller says, walking up behind us.

"Just exchanging condolences with your wife."

29

"You going to take Alfie for a walk before bed?" Mary says when she sees me putting on my jacket and tucking my watch cap into my back pocket.

"I thought I would," I says.

Alfie's up and standing at my knee, ready, willing, and raring to go.

"I'll maybe be an hour or even a little bit more," I says. "I thought I'd show Alfie the whole neighborhood in case he ever gets out one day and has to find his way home. Maybe we'll stroll all the way down to the river."

"Where are you going, Jimmy?" Mary says, giving me the eye.

"I told Willy Dink I'd meet him around the corner and tell him how I was doing about getting his creatures out of the pound."

"That's all you're going to do?"

"That's all I had in mind."

"So, how did you do at the pound?"

"Not sensational. They made a price. If Willy Dink paid it, he'd have to sell his truck and go out of business."

A little sympathy frown pops up between her pretty eyes.

"And that's all you're going to do for an hour, maybe a little more?"

"Well, I thought . . ."

"I don't want to know. If you tell me what you have in mind, I'll only worry. So don't tell me. Just be careful."

"I got Alfie to watch out for me," I says.

Alfie tries to look mean and trots out the door and down the stairs alongside me like he's carrying my sword.

Willy Dink's sitting on the running board of his truck, waiting for me. His yellow eyes are shining, reflecting the dim light of the streetlamp. I wonder can he see in the dark.

"Hello, Mr. Flannery," he says. "How do we stand?"

"Not so good. They want six hundred dollars."

He whooshes with his lips like a radiator valve letting go. Then he reaches out and scratches Alfie behind the ear.

"Nice pup," he says.

"We get along," I says.

"So I guess that's that," Willy Dink says, getting up with great effort and limping around to the driver's side of the cab.

"You hurt your leg?" I says.

He gives me a look like what kind of a man am I not to understand somebody can limp from a wound to the spirit just like he can from an injury to the body. He drags himself up behind the wheel like he'll never be himself again.

"Can this machine go over twenty miles an hour?" I says, jumping in beside him.

"It can do plenty," he says.

"Let's go, Alfie," I says, and Alfie jumps on my lap.

"Get over to Maywood. Don't get stopped by a cop, but don't drag your foot either."

"What are we going to do?" he says.

"We're going to spring your chicken," I says.

Willy Dink knows more back roads without traffic lights and cops than Dunleavy. We're over to Maywood and the Animal Control pound in half the time it took me. I tell him to cut his engine when we're half a block away and coast in close, but not too close, to the main building, over where there's some heavy shadows.

Alfie starts to tremble when he gets a whiff of the dogs and cats. He looks at me like he's asking me did I change my mind and am I tossing him back into the soup. I give him a hug and he licks my nose. He's not scared anymore.

There's some industrial lights outside the building, but there ain't lights shining out from inside fronting on the parking area, and the ones they have got are pretty dim.

"You got a hat?" I says.

Willy Dink reaches back and takes a greasy old felt from behind the seat.

"No, one something like this," I says, taking out the knitted watch cap and pulling it down over my face.

"I ain't got nothing like that," he says. "How could I see walking around like that?"

I poke my fingers where the eyeholes should be, taking it off and cut them out with my penknife.

"Like that," I says, "I tried talking your animals out of there. I tried bribing them out for a reasonable price. Now, we're going to set them free."

"My God, you'd break the law to help me?"

"It don't mean I'm in love with you, Willy Dink, so don't remind me again or I might have second thoughts."

He reaches back and comes up with one of them big cardboard buckets for taking out chicken dinners.

"My supper," he says, borrowing my knife and cutting out eyeholes for hisself.

He turns it upside down and jams it down over his ears. Lucky he's got such a small head or it'd never fit.

I put my ruined watch cap back and pull it down to my neck.

"You stay here, Alfie. Anybody comes you give us the word. Okay?"

I swear he practically nods.

"We could be sneaky and look for a way in," I says as Willy Dink and me walk up to the front door, "but, I tell you, I don't think this calls for sneaky. It calls for bold."

"Whatever you say, *mon capitaine,*" he says.

"Give me a break, Willy Dink," I says. "This ain't a movie. This is serious business."

Henry Hackinaw is sitting behind the counter with his feet up and a book in his lap. He's fast asleep with his mouth open. I can see a wad of chewing gum caught in the well of his lip.

I give Willy Dink the finger on the lip and we tiptoe over to the door that goes into the hall with all the cages. I got my hand on the knob and I stick my mouth up close to Willy's cardboard bucket.

"Once we get inside," I says in a whisper, "we got to be fast. You get Timmy, Max, and Hershel. I'll get the chicken, the armadillo, and the raccoon."

"I better . . ."

I grab his arm. Trying to whisper inside the bucket is a waste of time. His voice booms out like he's using a megaphone. Hackinaw stirs but don't wake up.

Willy Dink takes off the bucket and says, "I better take Shirley."

"Who?"

"The raccoon. She can be very mean with strangers."

"Okay, then I'll take Timmy. We'll gather them up and go out the other end of the building to the breeze-way. Ready?"

"Ready."

"Put your bucket back on."

Just like I figure, the minute I open the door and we step inside, the dogs are awake and raising hell. If any-body pulls up outside and Alfie *does* give the warning, who could hear it?

I hit the lights and some brights go on. I point to the small cages. "There's your snake and your raccoon," I says, while I'm opening up another cage and snatching out the armadillo. I grab the chicken next, which lets out a terrible squawk and gives me a shot on the nose.

"You dumb chicken," I says, "I'm trying to save your life."

It flies out of the cage and lands on my shoulder, digging its claws into me like I'm a roost in a henhouse. I see Willy Dink's got his snake around his neck, his ferret on his shoulder, and is just picking up his raccoon like she was a baby. I tuck the armadillo under my arm like a football and run down to the end where Timmy's in his cage. I stoop down and open it up. He rushes out and bites me on the ankle just to let me know he ain't forgiven or forgot that I left him to sweat it out a whole day.

The door by the office slams open. Hackinaw yells, "Hey, you!"

I look back and there's Willy Dink just finishing up opening every cage he can get his paws on. The place is swarming with dogs and cats, every one of them looking for a way out. I open the door to the breezeway and run. Willy Dink's right behind me. And this pack of dogs and cats is all around us, getting under our feet.

We get to the truck and pile in, Willy Dink's animals in the back, except for Timmy, who hops in the front and gives Alfie the evil eye.

"Move," I says, shoving Timmy over. Alfie jumps in my lap and looks at Timmy like he's saying, "It's your truck but this is my human."

We get out of there fast.

Willy Dink lets me off in front of the house and thanks me.

Mary's waiting up. She sees the torn leg on my trousers and the smear of blood on my sock. "What happened to you?" she says.

"One of the condemned prisoners I saved bit me."

30

I read a lot. All kinds of books. You'd be surprised.

What it seems to me is that the big thinkers are always trying to figure out what's normal about this or that so they got something to build their theories on.

I can understand that. I mean how can you figure if the problem of illegitimate babies is getting worse without you know how many there was last year, or ten years, or fifty years ago?

How do you know if you're losing ground, gaining ground, or running dead even without you know how much a man in your job made last year, ten years, fifty years ago?

Of course you got to figure in inflation, deflation, stagflation, and a different mix in the basket of commodities what makes up the standard-of-living index, or the cost-of-living index, or the gross-national-product report.

You've also got to reckon in when something becomes a necessity and ain't a luxury anymore. Like a telephone, or a television set, or tires with fifty-thousand-mile guarantees.

It gets very complicated and, even if you can work your way through it and come up with a number, what're you going to do with the number you got?"

I mean you tell a young woman with five kids and no husband, a buck in her pocket, and no roof over her head that she's the result of a shift in the kind of choices society is making, she's got every right to scream in your face and cry on your tie.

It looks to me like society, whatever you want to call the whole bunch of us, lives and acts according to charts and graphs what tell us something about these trends they keep talking about, but every single one of us lives from one good-luck day to the next bad-luck day, from a good experience to a bad experience. You ask a fella how's he doing and it all depends on what foot he's standing on.

"You take murder," I says out loud.

Alfie looks at me, ready to listen. It's morning and we're going over to Morgan and West Washington. It makes me feel good having somebody to talk to.

"I mean what's average when it comes to murder? You look at it one way, you got to admit that anyone commits murder, I mean willful homicide, has got to be off his tree. Right? Even if you kill somebody in a fit of temper, you got to say you was crazy when you done it. Right? Now, there's all kinds of *circumstances*. There's like diminished capacity which means you could be crazy with drink, crazy with drugs, or just plain crazy. There's provocation. This sucker what you blow away is pushing you and pushing you, or he's attacking your wife, or hurting your kid. And you see red. You go a little nuts. There's self-defense. Even then, I got to say, you're probably crazy with fear. So if crazy is a defense for committing murder, everybody convicted of it should be put in a hospital, nobody should ever go to jail, let alone be executed. You understand what I'm getting at?"

Alfie gives a little whine and leans up against the door because he figures this could be a long conversation.

I reach over and hit the button. I don't think he's heavy enough but, you never know, he could lean against the handle and go flying out the door.

"What I'm getting at," I says, while I'm pulling in to the curb by the old Rullin mansion in which there's this hologram museum, "is you kill somebody one day, they hit you with the book, you kill twenty the next and they say you ain't responsible."

I crack the window so Alfie can have some fresh air. I lock my side after I get out. Not, I don't think, that anyone would try to get into my car with Alfie sitting there. He can look very mean when he wants to.

I go to the front door. There's a brass plate that says "Museum of Holography. Please ring bell."

I do like it says and after a minute a young woman wearing tight jeans, high heels, and a man's shirt tied above her belly button comes down a short flight of marble steps to the entrance and opens up.

"You want to see the pictures?" she says.

She's got a hard face with knowing eyes and a red, greedy mouth. Her bleached hair's so stiff with lacquer it looks like a scouring pad.

"Are they worth seeing?" I says.

"Well, it's three dollars. You got to make up your mind is it worth it."

"Do I pay you now?"

She smiles, which softens her face a little. "You can come in first, if you want." She opens the door wider and lets me slip past. "But no free peeks."

I know this type of Chicago girl. She was raised in the streets with a drunk father and a wore-out mother. She's just pretty enough to have the men after her from the time she's fourteen, dumb enough to play to their weakness, smart enough not to give it away, tough enough to go it alone, hopeful enough to figure the prince will come along someday, and just confused enough to choose a good-looking toad when her turn comes to pick.

We walk up the steps to the landing. The reception hall is all paneled in dark wood. There's a staircase that goes sweeping up to the next floor. You can almost see old man Rullin, one of the meat barons, coming up to the mahogany table in the morning and picking up his mail off a silver tray.

Over to one side there's a little office carved out by a long glass-topped counter. There's a desk and chair and some filing cabinets behind it back alongside tall windows.

I go up to the counter to give her the three dollars and she gives me a ticket which she rips in half, giving me one piece and putting the other in a little green metal box.

Under the glass, is all these key rings, money clips, and little frames laid out on a black cloth. One of them is an eye you'd swear was floating six inches in the air.

"You want to see that?" she says.

"Sure."

She slides back the door, takes out the eye, and puts it on the counter. I tilt it back and forth between my fingers. You look at it one way it's a slightly rounded piece of plastic. You tilt it another and this eye comes up like it's really there, except it's greeny-gold instead of flesh-colored. When I hold it closer, I can see every little eyelash and the tears what keep the eyeball wet.

"I seen this eye somewheres before," I says.

"Oh, yeah?" she says.

I look up and wink. "Tell me the truth, is this your eye?"

She grins. "No, that ain't my eye. But I know the photographer what took the picture of that eye."

"I knew I saw you before. You used to work for Jerry has the studio down the block."

"You know Jerry Miller?" she says, something I can't read flickering in her expression for a second.

"Sure, I know Jerry," I says.

"You a friend of his?"

"I wouldn't say that."

"What would you say?"

"I'd say that speaking of eyes Jerry Miller's got very funny eyes."

She lets out a breath. "The creepiest."

"Very weird," I says.

"That ain't all," she says.

"How's that?"

"Don't you know?"

"Know what?"

She wants to tell me a story, but she wants me to work for it. "Well, if you don't know . . ." she says.

I give her my best crooked grin. "If you ask me don't I know, there's a million things I could maybe not know."

"If you knew this, you'd know what I was talking about "

"There's creepy and there's creepy," I says. "If you give me a hint . . ."

"The black room," she says.

"You mean his darkroom?"

"I don't mean the one where he develops the film. I mean the other one."

"Look," I says. "I don't know about any black room. I just told you that I ain't Miller's friend. I just came up a couple of times to make a delivery."

"It's funny I don't remember somebody like you. I mean the red hair."

"I know you mean the red hair. Everybody looks at the red hair, nobody looks at the face. Maybe I was wearing a hat. Sometimes I wear a hat."

She tries to imagine me with a hat. "No. I'd even remember if you was wearing a hat. What was you delivering?"

"Photographs of models."

"You work for an agency?" she says, brightening up and preening a little. Once upon a time somebody who was trying to get into her panties told her she should be a movie actress or a model and she never forgot it.

"I used to. Now and then. It was a part-timer."

"Oh," she says like I busted her balloon

"Was you a model?" I says.

"I done a little. That's why I was working over to

Jerry's at the reception desk. He promised to do a little something for me."

"You don't have to tell me."

"Tell you what?"

"What he was going to *do* for you. I mean with them eyes of his."

"You don't know the half of it. I mean, if a little . . . friendliness was all he wanted, I'm not saying I wouldn't have."

"Favor for favor."

"As long as a girl don't throw it around. You know what I mean?"

"You want to get along you got to go along?"

"That's it exactly. But that creep was definitely not into your straight everyday . . . though enjoyable . . . favor."

"What was he into?"

"You ever heard of necrophilia?"

"How's that?" I says.

"I don't blame you. I had to look it up for myself even after he told me what it was. I mean he told me what this necrophilia was and said he didn't have it because he didn't want his women dead, just laying still."

"I think I missed the train," I says.

"He wanted me to *pretend* like I was dead. Now, do you get my meaning?"

"I got an inkling."

"He's got this room painted black. Black floor, black walls, black ceiling. In the middle of the floor's this round couch covered in blood-red velvet. It's lit by a dim spotlight. There's pictures on the walls of people mangled up in car wrecks and people chopped up with axes. That coo-coo-monga asks me to take off all my clothes and lay down on the couch. He tells me I shouldn't move a muscle. Not a muscle."

"So what did you do?"

She looks at me, sorting out her options. She can tell

me a lie and end this nice little chat we're having on a boring morning. Or she can maybe tell me a different lie and see if she can keep me there so she can find out am I the prince, the toad, or whatever. Or she can tell me to mind my own business. There's a lot of ways to go and she's staring at me, making her choice.

"I told him no. What the hell you think I told him? I told him no and walked right out of there."

She's looking at me like she's trying to read my mind.

"And that's it?" I says, like a man who's just been told a joke without the punch.

"Welllll," she says.

"Yeah?" I says.

"Why should I be telling a stranger all about my private life?"

"My name's Jimmy Flannery," I says.

"Hey," she says, "I know you. You got my sister's rent paid for two months when her lousy old man ran out on her two winters ago and left her with two kids in a cold flat without a cent to her name."

"Look at that. We're practically friends . . . ?"

"Aurelia. Aurelia Chernick. My friends call me Ray."

"Nice to make your acquaintance, Ray," I says.

"Likewise," she says. Then she right away says, "He bribed me."

"Miller?"

"With a job at this catalog. Three weeks. Good money. It was a catalog for underwear, and underwear pays better. You know that?"

"Well, I should hope so," I says.

"So, I figured what the hell. Just the one time. What's so hard to lay still? I wouldn't do it today, you understand. What with AIDS and all. I wouldn't take the chance. Any man I take up with nowadays I got to have his pedigree, you understand, and even then he's got to wear a you-know-what."

"So you laid down on the couch . . ."

"First I made him take down them awful pictures and get some more lights in there. I wouldn't let him turn the organ music on either."

"I should hope not."

"The way it turned out, he couldn't do nothing after all. His thing wouldn't work. You know what I mean? He poked around a little, then he started to cry and said he ought to beat me up for spoiling things."

"The pictures off the walls."

"And the lights and no organ music. I told him he laid another hand on me, I'd see he was done and done good. I been threatened by tougher dudes than him. So he fired me."

"That was how long ago?"

"Maybe a year. Maybe a little more."

"I don't think he ever got another receptionist."

"Oh, he tried to get another one. More than one."

"What happened?"

"I fixed him. I'd just call up and if a woman answered I'd ask was she the new receptionist and if she said yes I'd tell her she should have a look behind the locked door before she settled in for a long career. He gave up trying lately."

So, I knew why Ray'd told me the story just like that. She'd tell the story to anybody who said they knew Miller. He'd threatened her and scared her and she'd never forget. She'd take a shot at him every chance she could.

"That girl what was found dead over in Kropotkin's building?"

"Yes," I says.

"She knew Jerry pretty good. He took her picture. In fact there's a picture of her right inside."

The phone rings and Ray picks up.

I take the chance to go look at the holograms.

There's a couple that are really something. They're like the colored outlines of mountains and rivers. When you look at them the right way they seem to float in midair like 3-D Chinese landscapes. There's a couple on revolving drums. On one of them a girl winks at you and turns her head, and on another she blows you a kiss.

There's a series of portraits on one wall. I come up on them from the side so they look like a bunch of shiny yellowish film in frames. But when I move around front on the first one Joyce Lombardi's face comes out of the picture frame at me.

It's so real I jerk my head back. Even the color is almost natural. I go closer and closer, staring at the lips and how they're parted so I can see some of her white teeth. If I move my head a little this way, a little that way, I can see the side of her nose and the corner of one eye and then the other. I can see her earrings glittering from inside the waves of her hair.

It's very quiet in the gallery. All I can hear is the whisper of the electric motors that turn the animated holograms round and round.

The room is black with just these low-level spotlights shining on the different pictures. Shining on Joyce's face and the faces of these other beautiful young women. Two of them got dark hair and one's a redhead. I seen their faces before. In the little pile of portraits on Miller's studio. If I ask him, I know he'll say, sure, that's why he's got them separated out. He was getting a brochure ready to announce this exhibition of his work at the museum. Something like that.

I go back to Joyce's face again. It does something to me. It's like she wants to whisper secrets to me and if I can get close enough her lips'll move and she'll tell me what I want to know.

When I was a kid about eleven a friend of mine down the block died of pneumonia one spring. It was the first funeral I ever went to. I remember looking down into his face as I knelt on the prayer stool and folded my hands under my chin. All of a sudden I had this awful feeling he was going to reach out from the coffin and touch me. I knew he was dead, I could tell from the way he looked, but I just knew he was going to touch me.

That's the way I feel now all of a sudden. That's the way Joyce looks. Except her eyes ain't closed the way his eyes was closed. Her eyes are open. There's something very funny about them. It takes me a minute to figure out what it is. They ain't wet with tears. They're dull and dry. Joyce looks dead in the picture because she is dead. She was dead when it was taken.

31

I ask Ray can I use the phone and make a call to Harold Boardman. He answers all my questions about the condition of dead eyes and tells me other awful things I don't even ask about.

Then I call the station and ask for Pescaro. While I'm waiting for him to get on the line I ask Ray what she can tell me about Miller's show of pretty women inside.

"What do you mean?" she says.

"Like when was it hung?"

"They've all been up for a long time," she says. "Except for Joyce. He put that up just the other day."

"What day was that?"

She thinks about it. "The day after she turned up dead on the front page of the newspaper."

Pescaro gets on the phone. I tell him where I am and where I'm going to be in ten minutes. I also tell him why. Then I hang up the phone. My hands are sweating and I wipe them off on my handkerchief.

Ray's looking at me wide-eyed.

"You told that cop that Jerry Miller killed Joyce Lombardi?" she says.

"Also them other three women in there."

"You going over there alone?"

"Well, I hope I ain't going to be alone for long."

She hugs herself like she's got a sudden chill. "Hey," she says.

I don't say anything.

"I could've been one of the pictures in his gallery."

"Keep taking care of yourself," I says, and go down the stairs to the door.

When I get to the second floor of Kropotkin's building, there's a sign on Miller's door what says "Back in 10 minutes." People put out signs that say ten minutes and come back in half an hour. It could be he left a minute ago or nine minutes ago. I had this idea in my head how I'd go into his outer office without a receptionist, turn on the intercom, go into wherever he's working, get the intercom in there turned on, confront him with what I think, and have Pescaro and his boys out in the other room listening to his confession. You work up a plan like that on the spur of the moment, off the top of your head, and usually it ain't much of a plan.

I go downstairs through the basement and take the flight of stairs in the back up to the studio. I go through the darkroom to the locked door and slip it with a credit card.

The black room with the blood-red couch and the terrible pictures on the wall is there just like Ray said it was. A couple of the pictures has been knocked off the wall. There's broken glass all over the floor.

"I knew you were bad news the minute I laid eyes on you," Miller says at my back.

"I got an old friend says you should never trust a man who walks too soft," I says, turning around to face him.

He's standing there with a glass in his hand. "You even got nosy about me with my wife at a funeral. Haven't you got any shame?"

"You always got a drink in your paw?" I says.

"How's that?"

"You left a glass in Joyce's apartment the night she was murdered. Then you went and got it back when the cops were in Scanlan's."

"How'd I do that without going past Scanlan's door?"

"Up the back stairs the same way I got in here."

"That'd just put me in the hall."

"I guess you got a key. Everybody seems to have a key."

He smiles at me. "Why don't you get the hell out of here before I call the cops and charge you with breaking and entering?"

I look around at the awful pictures on the wall. "Because I think maybe you want to talk."

"No, I don't want to talk."

"About Joyce, I mean. Don't you want to talk about Joyce?"

I know the look on Miller's face and in his eyes. I seen it before in the eyes and faces of people who're carrying around some terrible burden and want to confess their sins.

Years ago, Father Mulrooney, over to St. Pat's, could always tell when I had something preying on my mind. At least I thought he could. Maybe it was just that he knew that practically everybody in the world has something preying on their mind and all you got to do is talk soft, show them a little concern, and they'll break down and spill the beans.

"Were you the boyfriend she busted up with?" I says like my words are in his own head. "Was Frazier just the sugar daddy?" I says, not believing what I'm saying even a little bit, just trying to find a crack where I can drive a wedge and get him talking.

For a minute his funny eyes brighten up. I can see he likes the idea. For a minute he thinks about going along with my suggestion, building himself a reputation for being a great ladies' man right on the spot. Then his eyes go flat and he shakes his head, looking down at his glass, remembering all his failures and the sickness that drives him.

"Charlie Frazier was her boy," he says, shaking his head as though he can't figure out why. "You ever meet him? He's like something out of a waxworks. How come he's got it all and had Joyce too?"

"Some people got luck. Some people ain't. You ain't had much luck, have you?"

Miller walks past me and sits down on the couch, the glass in both hands, his arms on his knees, looking up at me. "What the hell are you talking about?"

"I'm talking about how a man can feel like such a loser he tries to prove himself on top of women. If he still feels like a loser, he beats them up or maybe wants them to lay still and let him use them. And if that don't work he wants them dead."

He's staring at me like he's looking to see if there's disgust showing my face. I hope it ain't showing. All I want him to see is that I'm trying to love the sinner even though I hate the sin.

"How did it happen? Were you waiting for her in her place?" I says.

He shakes his head. "She knocked on my door. She wanted to say good-bye."

"She told you she was leaving her apartment for good?"

"Leaving the apartment and leaving Charlie Frazier."

"How did that make you feel? Happy?"

"Sure. Why should a sonofabitch like Frazier have everything and Joyce too?"

"Did you ask her where she was going?" I says. When he don't answer I says, "Did she tell you she was moving in with a woman?"

He nods.

"Did she tell you what kind of a relationship it was going to be?"

He stares at me. "Not at first."

"How did you get her to take her clothes off?" I says.

"I asked her to let me take her picture for my show across the street."

"For friendship's sake?"

"For cash. I told her I'd pay her. I told her that she'd

better pick up every buck she could without Frazier to pay the bills for her anymore."

"So she took off her clothes?"

"Just her blouse and bra because she decided to wash her hair if she was going to let me take her picture."

"When did you strangle her?"

"She was drying her hair with a hand dryer she had in her bag," he says, not like he's answering my question but like he's talking to himself. "She said if she hadn't come back for it she wouldn't even have stopped in to say good-bye to me, because she was feeling very down on men. She said she was disgusted with them. She said she was going to try women for a while. The way she said it it was like she wanted to stick a knife in me."

"She didn't mean you in particular."

"I know that. That just made it worse. It was like she didn't even think of me like I was a man. She was standing there half-naked, with just a towel around her shoulders, looking in the mirror, putting these earrings back in her ears. I was standing in the doorway behind her and she looked into my eyes in the mirror and told me she'd rather make love to a woman than to me."

"To men," I correct him very softly. "So you tried to make love to her and she wouldn't have it."

"I asked her what a beautiful girl like her was doing throwing herself away on a dyke."

He keeps staring at me, his eyes never moving. His face is like a mask. Like one of them pictures of the dead women over in the museum. Just his lips move when he speaks. Move just a little bit.

"How did she take that?" I says.

"She asked me did I think it would be better for a beautiful girl like her to throw herself away on a creep like me who sniffed around like a dog but wouldn't be able to do anything if she said yes."

"You'd tried and failed before?"

"No. I lied about that. We never. She knew about my

problem because my wife let it drop. My wife Connie's very good at letting things like that drop."

"So then you killed Joyce. You took her picture after she was dead. Then you put her in the dumbwaiter and lifted her up to Scanlan's, where you put her on his bed while you thought about how to get rid of her. You knew that Scanlan was supposed to be gone another week."

Pescaro, O'Shea, and Rourke appear in the doorway.

"Are those cops standing behind me?" Miller says.

"That's right," I says.

"So what have we got?" Miller says, smiling at me.

"We got the man who killed Joyce Lombardi and three other women, then tried to rape them and took their pictures instead."

"No, what we've got is a couple of acquaintances sitting in a room fixed up for a photo spread, having a little chat, making up stories. You haven't got a thing that would stand up in court."

"We've got Joyce's hologram you just hung up on the wall across the street."

"I made that portrait a long time ago."

"The earrings she was wearing when you killed her will prove otherwise."

32

When these things is over they never feel like they're over.

Scanlan's out of jail and back in his apartment.

Frazier sends me an invitation to sit at the big affair where he's going to officially kick off his campaign for governor, which has been going on for more than half a year already. I send back my regrets.

Kropotkin gets in touch with me to ask me to get Janet Canarias to put in a word over to the Historical Society so his building'll get on the register. He says he's going to need all the help he can get because it's going to be that much harder renting apartments in a building in which there was a murder and a murderer.

When I go over to ask the favor, Janet and me talk for maybe twenty minutes. Her thoughts wander three times. I don't have to ask her what she's thinking about.

I'm sitting on the stoop thinking that what's over should feel like it's over, so everybody can get on with it, the way we got to do, when Willy Dink drives up in his truck.

"They done it to me again, Flannery," he says. "They stole my crew. That Oscar Lukakis hunted me down and stole my pets."

"We got them out once, Willy Dinks, I don't think we could pull the same stunt twice."

"So?"

"So, you got to come up with six hundred bucks."

"They upped the ante on me. Now, what with this fine and that penalty, and threats of prosecution, the price's gone up to a thousand."

"This is getting out of hand," I says. "Grab your sack and come with me."

We go down into the sewers to a spot I know where the rats congregate. It takes Willy Dink maybe an hour to trap and bag a dozen big beauties. We drive down to City Hall with this squirming bag. We go up to Dunleavy's offices and find a spot to dump the rats off. Then Willy Dink and me go sit and wait on the stairs right by the door to Streets and Sanitation.

It don't take long before we hear this scream what rattles the windows.

"We'll give it another five minutes," I says.

We hear three more screams before the time is up.

"Let's go," I says. We get up and walk through the door and up to the counter. Dunleavy's people are milling around, grabbing up phones. All of a sudden Dunleavy hisself appears in a doorway shouting, "Get Jimmy Flannery down here right away!" Then he spots me standing there with Willy Dink.

He charges toward me, through the swinging door, and grabs my arm. "There's two rats as big as ponies in my office," he says. "Do you know how to get in touch with that—"

"Willy Dink," I says.

"—rat catcher with the snakes and weasels?"

Then he eyes Willy Dink. "Don't tell me," Dunleavy says. "This is the man."

"Like a blessing from heaven," I says.

Dunleavy's no fool but he's in distress and needs immediate relief.

"Then tell him to get his beasts and go to work," Dunleavy says.

"Well, you see, Mr. Dunleavy," I says. "My friend Willy Dink has this little problem. It's something which a man like yourself can take care of with the wave of a hand."

It ain't long after that when Willy Dink's put on the city payroll to take care of any unusual problems of vermin or rodent infestation.